When Frank, the hero of *You're Thinking About Doughnuts*, has ?
to go on a school trip to a stately home, it doesn't occur
to him that the objects on display will come alive. But
that is exactly what happens.

Frank is just looking at the picture of the eighteenth-
century family and their young black servant, when she
steps out of the picture and tells Frank that her name is
"Not-Sheba". The girl wants to find out her real African
name and Frank agrees to help her out. In the course of
their wanderings Frank and the girl meet a celebrity-
mad mummy, who is desperate to be a star, some
statues from India and exploited Vistorian workers.
And of course they all are determined to tell Frank
their stories.

Another witty, zany story from Michael Rosen.

MICHAEL ROSEN

You're Thinking About Tomatoes

Decorations by Quentin Blake

BARN OWL BOOKS

First published in 2005 by Barn Owl Books
157 Fortis Green Road, London N10 3LX
Barn Owl Books are distributed by Frances Lincoln
4 Torriano Mews, Torriano Avenue, London NW5 2RZ

ISBN 1-903015-44-8

Designed and typeset by Douglas Martin
Printed in the UK by
Cox & Wyman Ltd, Reading, Berkshire

TO JOE AND EDDIE –
WHO HELPED ME WRITE IT

CONTENTS

Chapter 1

Thinking About a Tomato

Frank watched the head teacher's lips moving. He could hear that he was speaking. He knew that he was being told off. What he didn't know was what Mr Butcher was getting at, exactly. There was quite a lot about how "disappointed" he was, his mother was mentioned quite often but the rest was a blur: ". . . if you don't buck up . . . I'm not the only one to be saying this . . . what are we all here for, eh? . . some things in life aren't nice, they're necessary . . . you've fallen right behind, lad . . . you're a dreamer, boy, a dreamer . . ."

Frank was thinking about Mr Butcher's chin. It was like a little tomato, he thought, all round and red and shiny. *I wonder what would happen if I stuck a pin in it?* "... some of the complaints I've had are very serious ..." *Would it burst?* "... you're in a dream, boy, you're in a drea ..." *Maybe it would collapse like a flat tyre, pheeeeee, and then finish with a blowing raspberry sound.*

"Can you hear what I'm saying to you, Frank? Frank?"

"Yessir!"

"Have you been listening to what I'm saying?"

"Yessir!"

"What have I been saying?"

"Er ..." The tomato kept bobbing about in front of him. He wanted to say, *"Tomatoes, sir. You've been talking about tomatoes."*

"Well?"

Frank searched around in his head for something that he had heard Mr Butcher say.

All he could find was: "I've got to buck up, sir."

It wasn't enough for Mr Butcher. "Yes, Frank, yes – and a good deal more. Well, listen to this, my boy, and this you'd better remember ..."

This I'd better remember, thought Frank.

"Your mother wants you to go to the City High School, am I right?"

"Yessir!"

"Do you want to go there?"

"I don't know, sir."

"No, I'm sure you don't. But your mother is quite sure. And she knows and I know what this means. Do you know?"

"No, sir."

"I'm sure you don't."

He said that a moment ago, thought Frank.

"Well, I'll tell you." *I'm sure you will,* thought Frank. "I have to recommend you. Do you know what that means?"

Oh, this is really tiring, thought Frank. *It gives me brain ache.* Mr Butcher didn't wait for him to answer this time. "It means . . ." *Ooh, I'd love to squeeze that tomato chin till the pips burst out.* "It means . . . that you have to work, work, work. You've got to convince me that you've got application, that you can knuckle down and stick at it. The City High School is not for flashy little fellas with the odd spark of brightness in their heads. They want to know that you can start a job, and carry on a job, and finish a job. You, Frank, start rarely; carry on once in a blue moon; and finish NEVER."

The last 'NEVER' took so much out of Mr Butcher that he had to stop and do a little breathing and have a rub of his tomato for a moment or two. There was an awkward pause so Frank thought he ought to say something. "Yessir!" said Frank without having the tiniest idea of what he was saying 'yes' to.

"Right – you have one last chance. Tomorrow, your class is going to Chiltern House. I have prepared a worksheet for you. This means that you've got to work. It's not going to be just any run-of-the-mill, ordinary school outing. Chiltern House is a very old and famous place full of fascinating and exciting things."

Oh no, thought Frank, *not another of those fascinating places that turn out to be so boring that you want to sit down and sleep for a year.*

"I want that worksheet filled in, completed, in my hand by the time you climb back on to the coach in the Chiltern House car park. If it's not, you can say goodbye to the City High

School, and, as far as I'm concerned you're on the scrap heap, a waste, with no future – nothing. Now, is there anything else you want to say for yourself?"

Can I stick a pin in your chin, sir? No, he didn't say it. Instead, a picture came up in Frank's mind of the thousands of kids at the other schools – Hill End, Downton and Sir Nigel Lancaster's – in a huge scrap heap, with a great crane dropping more and more kids on the top. Was that true? Were all those kids just scrap?

"Well?"

"It's a big scrap heap, sir," said Frank.

"That's right, and you want to make sure you're not on it. Now off you go and back to your class. Remember, tomorrow's your last chance."

Frank walked out of Mr Butcher's study, past the football shield, the netball cup, the handicraft goblet, the perseverance medal and the excellence clock. *I won't get any of those,* said Frank to himself.

No Shouting, No Running . . .

The coach pulled up in the car park.

"I want your attention please," said Mr Butcher. "That is all of you, Robert, all of you . . . I'm waiting. I'm not going to shout. It doesn't make any difference to me if we stay in the car park all day. I've been here many times before but as far as you're concerned, no one, no one at all is going to leave this coach until I have your attention. When —"

"Can I go to the toilet, sir?"

"No you can NOT. You had a chance to use the school toilets before we left and there'll be plenty of chances to use the Chiltern House toilets ALL DAY."

"Dave's drink's leaked, sir."

"Would you come out from under that seat, Rasheda?"

"Hey, wow, look at that park over there, it's got one of them assault thingies."

"I don't mind waiting." Mr Butcher pretended to be massively interested in a tree. "I really don't. As far as I'm concerned, I can sit here, listen to the radio, eat my sandwiches and enjoy the view. I didn't come here for my good . . . right . . . thank you. Now, Chiltern House is a very old house and it's very famous, put that down Joe. The very oldest parts were built eight hundred years ago no one, no one at all is going to start their lunch NOW, is that understood?

"Today Chiltern House belongs to everyone, but for hundreds of years it belonged to the Chiltern family why are you fiddling with your bag? I've said no one is going to eat their lunch now, so there's no need to be fiddling with YOUR BAG, IS THERE? The way you're going on, son, you won't be getting off this coach, I can tell you.

"Now Chiltern House is bigger than any house any of you have ever been in before. Every room is full of very valuable and beautiful things, Pauline, very valuable and beautiful things, Pauline. Pauline, what have I just said? Mmm? Don't tell her, Tracey. No of course you don't know, Pauline. You can see me later.

"We want every one of you to get the most out of this visit. We want you to look and learn, don't we, Frank? What do we want?"

"You want us to look and learn, sir."

"Good Lord, Frank's awake. We've prepared a worksheet for you. That noise was completely uncalled for, thank you very much. The worksheet — is that a mobile you've got there, Darren? And what precisely do you think you'll be doing in Chiltern House with a mobile? Ordering a pizza? That'll be staying on the coach, I can tell you. The worksheet is a quiz, heavens above, Keeley, you've got eight hundred years of history to take pictures of and you're using up film on Davina's face — WHILE I'M TALKING.

"If I have to interrupt myself once more, we're turning round and going back. I mean it. I mean it. When we get inside, that's not a joke, I'm hoping we will get inside if you kindly let me finish what I am saying . . . when we get inside, there are rules you have to follow. We learnt them in assembly yesterday morning. Let me hear them."

Everyone chanted: "No shouting, no running, no touching, no eating, no drinking, be polite at all times. Make sure you are *where* you should be, *when* you should be."

"Georgina, I didn't see your lips move once. Stay behind with me. Right, the rest of you, off you go. Mrs Morrell, will you hand out the worksheets please? Your timetable is at the top of your worksheet."

"What time do you want us back, sir?"

"George, I have said, at least I believe I have just said, less than four seconds ago: "YOUR TIMETABLE IS AT THE TOP OF THE WORK-SHEET." What do you think that means?"

"It means that at the top of my worksheet, er, there's a timetable."

"And what does that mean?"

"I don't understand, sir."

"Well, I'll explain to you, George, and to anyone else who doesn't understand. The timetable tells you where to be and when. This means that you don't have to ask questions like: "What time do you want us back, sir?" It's all there, on the timetable, ON THE WORKSHEET, George. Clever, isn't it? We may not be geniuses, but we think we know what we're doing. I hope we're good enough for you, George. Right, off you go."

The children tumbled out of the coach, collected their worksheets and charged across the car park to Chiltern House.

Chapter 3

A Girl out of a Picture

Frank stared at the sheets of paper. The work-sheet. There seemed to be hundreds of questions: When was this? Why was that? How old is that? How many of these? What is the name of this? Who is the that? Why do you think this?

He turned the sheets over. There were gaps. Draw this. Show that. What can you see in this place? Draw it. He turned over some more pages. Imagine you are this. Write what you think this person might have thought about that . . . *It was going to take weeks to fill it in. You could stay in Chiltern House a whole year and you wouldn't be able to do it all.* Frank began to feel nervy. It mattered so much, Mr Butcher had said.

He became aware of everyone around him rushing off in all directions with their pencils and pens and felt tips at the ready. *They all seem to know what they have to do — and even worse, they seem to be enjoying themselves.* Frank looked around him. Mr Butcher was talking to a man in uniform; Mrs Morrell was walking off with Keeley and Davina. They were in a huge, high room, with massive pictures on the wall. There was a long, shiny floor and lengths of thick blue rope strung from post to post, marking off chairs and tables and old wooden boxes round the edge of the room.

Mr Butcher was at his shoulder. "Press on, Frank. Press on. This place is hundreds of years old. It's full of history. Jam-packed full of it. Get your head down, lad, and learn a thing or two."

Frank wandered off, staring around him. He ran his fingers along the blue rope as he stared at the huge pictures. He strolled off into another room, just as high, just as long, and then into another with more chairs, more huge pictures and more blue rope. He remembered the worksheet in his hand and looked down at it again. Why, when, where, what. He turned over the page. Draw, show, picture. He turned over another page. Imagine, write, imagine. He focused his eyes: "Find the picture of Lord Chiltern's children, Charlotte and William. Imagine you are one of them. Write your thoughts about living in Chiltern House using what you have learnt so far."

Frank felt a sagging feeling inside. He hadn't learnt anything 'so far'. He couldn't even *see* the picture of William and Charlotte, let alone imagine he was one of them. Out of the corner of his eye, he noticed there was a bench that wasn't sectioned off with blue rope. He sat down on it and stared in front of him.

He found himself gazing at another huge picture. There was a boy and a girl standing looking at him, wearing old-fashioned, frilly clothes. He could see the sign next to it. Yes, it said: 'Lord Chiltern's children: Charlotte and William'. Right, so all he had to do was imagine he was one of them. He stared at their faces. They looked slightly puffy, like pastries with too much stuffing inside.

Suddenly he heard a voice: "Get me out of here." Frank looked around. There was nobody there.

"Over here, I'm not invisible." It was a girl's voice. Frank looked again at Charlotte.

"No, not her. Everyone looks at her. Me. Over here."

Frank looked around again. Charlotte and William were standing in front of a table. Behind the table, in the dark, up against a curtain, standing sideways on, was somebody else. It was another girl.

"Yes, that's right – me," she said. "Get me out of here, will you?"

Frank started mumbling. "I don't – er – look, I'm not sure."

"Just keep looking at me, will you?"

"I am," said Frank.

"That's it, keep looking and I think that'll do it." Frank stared.

She began to move out of the shadows. She came round from behind the table and stepped out of the picture. "Ah, that's better," she said, "that's better," and stretched.

Frank went on staring at her.

"What's your name?" she said.

"Frank," said Frank.

"No one asks me asks me my name. They don't even see me," said the girl, "so they wouldn't, would they? They look at Miss Charlotte and Master William and then walk on."

"What's your name?" said Frank

"I don't know," said the little girl.

"There wasn't much point in my asking you then, was there?" said Frank.

"Oh, there's plenty of point. I ask myself nearly every day," said the girl.

"Look," said Frank, "actually I can't hang about. I've got this worksheet to fill in and if I don't finish it I'm for the scrap heap."

"I'm never on the worksheets," said the girl. "Let's have a look. Yes . . . yes . . . and yes, it's all dead easy. I could do that for you in about three minutes."

"Great," said Frank. "This is a real stroke of luck meeting you. DO it then."

"Not so fast, Scrapheap," said the girl pulling the worksheet out of Frank's reach. "We could come to a deal here. You help me find my name, I help with the worksheet."

23

"Find your name?" said Frank. "Don't be crazy. I can't even find out all that stuff on the worksheet, so how am I going to find out something as hard as your name?"

"You don't help me, you don't get your worksheet back."

Frank felt panicky. He could imagine Mr Butcher's face and chin boiling up: "You lost it, boy? You lost your worksheet? What did you do? Eat it? Eh? A girl took it off you? What girl? A girl who walked out of the picture, eh? Very believable. And what was her name? Oh, she didn't have a name? Really? Well, well, well. What do you think I am, lad? MAD? Do you expect me to believe a cock-and-bull story like that? Goodness me, Frank, you're in trouble this time. Serious trouble, believe me."

"OK," said Frank to the girl, "I'll help you," and he laughed very quietly inside, to himself. *How in heaven's name can I help anyone when I can't even help myself? But if it makes her happy, or, more to the point, if it makes her get going on the worksheet, good enough.*

"It's Sheba," said the girl.

"What?" said Frank.

"Sheba."

"What?" said Frank, "what's Sheba?"

"My name," said the girl.

"But you just said you didn't know your name."

"That's right."

"Then that's OK," said Frank. "I've helped you find your name, now you can do the worksheet."

"Not so fast. Sheba is what they call me. That's the name they gave me. But it's not my real name. Sheba was just a fancy name they thought up because they didn't want me to have my real name, did they?"

"No." said Frank, trying to look as though he understood what she was talking about. "I get it. They didn't want you to have your real, you know, NAME."

"So they called me Sheba – PAH!" said the girl crossly.

The only other time Frank had heard the name Sheba was Mrs Weston's cat.

"You know why they called me Sheba?" said the girl.

"After Mrs Weston's cat?" said Frank.

25

"Because it was the only posh name they could think of for a girl who was black."

"They could have called you Nadine," said Frank. "Nadine's in my class and she's black."

"But we're not talking about now, are we? I'm from two hundred and fifty years ago. There weren't any Nadines about then, you know."

"Sheba sounds all right to me," said Frank.

"It might be all right, but it's not my name, is it? It's only what Lord Chiltern called me when he brought me here."

"Right," said Frank.

"I wasn't born here, you know," said the girl.

"Weren't you?" said Frank, thinking it was really quite hard trying to understand anything that this girl was going on about. If only she'd stop trying to explain things and just get on with the worksheet, he'd feel a lot happier.

"Everyone else round here was white, weren't they? Look!" The girl pointed at all the pictures. There were earls and admirals and duchesses and generals and princes dressed in their grand uniforms, carrying swords, with battles going on behind them – and sure enough they were all white. "So I must have come from somewhere else, mustn't I? They kept saying I was their 'little Sheba' but I knew. They couldn't trick me I was their own daughter, or anybody else's daughter from round here. Trouble is, ever since I got stuck up here in this picture, I've never been able to get off again and find out where I came from. It's taken me a lot of figuring and a lot of thinking to get this far and I'm not going to let a chance like this go by."

"A chance like what?" said Frank. He was trying to follow, but it was all too difficult.

"I'm off. You got me out of the picture didn't you? So now you're going to help me. It's your fault for getting me out of there, there's nothing you can do about it now."

"Only if you help me with the worksheet."

The girl looked bothered for a moment. "Look, if there's the odd little thing I don't know the answer to, we'll ask someone else. I know everyone round here. We all shout to each other when there's no one here. Me stuck up there on the painting, everyone else in their glass cases in the other rooms. All shouting to each other. But some of them are a long way off. I don't know them very well," she said.

"So you don't know it all, do you?" said Frank. "You said you could do it dead easy, but actually there's loads of it you can't do. Is THAT what you mean?"

The girl kept the worksheet well out of Frank's reach. "Don't try anything, Scrapheap. I said I'll help you. Now you help me."

"Right," said Frank concentrating very hard on nothing at all. That was one thing he reckoned he was really good at.

"What do we do next?" said the girl.

"Right," said Frank.

"Can you stop saying 'right'?" said the girl.

"If you stop calling me Scrapheap," said Frank.

"Right," said the girl.

"Did you just say 'right'?" said Frank.

"Yes," said the girl.

"I thought you did," said Frank.

"It's not me that isn't allowed to say 'right'," said the girl, "it's you."

"Yes," said Frank, "I noticed. By the way, what do I call you?"

"Not Sheba, you can –"

"Not Sheba, Not-Sheba," said Frank, "That sounds good."

"You're going to call me Not-Sheba?" said the girl. "But my name's not Not-Sheba."

"I know," said Frank, "but I can't call you Frank, can I?"

"No," said the girl.

"So that leaves Not-Sheba," said Frank.

The girl seemed stuck for words for a moment.

"Who was Sheba anyway?" said Frank. "Apart from you, that is."

"Mrs Weston's cat," said Not-Sheba.

Chapter 4

The Curse of the Mummy's Tomb

Not-Sheba and Frank walked into a long, narrow room and stood looking about them.

Frank said, "I've really got to do this worksheet, you know, or I'm for it. If Mr Butcher catches me wandering about like this, I don't know what'll happen."

"Don't you like walking about with me?" said Not-Sheba in a teasing sort of voice. Frank blushed and looked the other way. More chairs, more tables, more blue rope. But where was everybody? Where was the rest of the class? And what was that noise?

"Did you hear that?" said Frank.

"I hear everything," said Not-Sheba, "that's all I've done for years: hear everything."

"Did you hear that creaking noise?" said Frank.

"Everything creaks around here," said Not-Sheba.

Frank looked towards where he thought the creak was coming from. It came from another part of the room, cordoned off with the blue ropes. There, instead of old chairs and tables were little statues. Frank walked slowly and carefully towards the rope and read the labels: there was a 'Chinese Goose', and an 'Ancient Egyptian Cat'. There were bits of– Then the creak happened again. Sounded like wood being split – a hard, vicious sort of noise, right close by. Frank stepped back and looked round for Not-Sheba. She had gone.

"Hey, where are you?" Frank called out. "You've got my worksheet!"

The creak creaked again. "What's going on?" Frank called out again. "Not-Sheba, where are you?" He suspected a plot: *Not-Sheba is ganging up with some nutter who's smashing the place up, and they're in with Mr Butcher, who's going to tell my Mum.*

Out of the corner of his eye, Frank saw a hand waving. It was coming from the great wide fireplace. A hand was poking down the chimney and waving. Frank felt horrible. He just stared at the hand. Then he realised whose hand it was: Not-Sheba's. She had dashed off to hide and had wedged herself upside down, half way up the chimney. She poked her upside-down head out of the chimney. "Quick, over here," she said.

Frank tiptoed backwards and joined her. *What does she know that I don't? Why is she so sure that it was such a good idea to rush off and hide?* "What's going on?" whispered Frank.

There was a pause.

She doesn't want to tell me, he thought. *It's a trick. The whole thing's a trick. I should never have gone along with this crazy business of trying to find out her name.* "What's going on?" said Frank again to the upside-down head.

"I don't know," said Not-Sheba.

She's lying, thought Frank.

The creak creaked loud and hard.

Frank was sure he saw something move this time. It came from the Chinese Goose. *Or was it the cat?*

Not-Sheba groaned.

32

"What's the matter?" said Frank.

"I'm scared," said Not-Sheba.

"*You're* scared?" said Frank. "You've lived here for hundreds of years, haven't you? I've never been here in my life and any minute now Mr Butcher's going to find me and I'm done for."

"Have you any idea what kind of trouble I'm in?" hissed Not-Sheba, still upside down. "When they find I'm not behind the table with Miss Charlotte and Master William, her ladyship will come for me with the end of the broom, beat me and then lock me in a room for a week." For one split second Frank found himself wondering why on earth Not-Sheba was worried about some weird stuff to do with a Miss This and a Master That and not so bothered about the horrible noise. Then:

Creak.

There it was again. It wasn't the goose or the cat. It was the mummy. The Egyptian mummy behind the cat. Frank and Not-Sheba moved closer together and stared as the mummy slowly cracked open like an egg. *Is that a hatching chick inside?* The wood splintered and creaked. From

33

the dark inside, there was a movement. First a hand and then an arm pushed its way out. It was grey and bandaged.

Frank turned away. "This is horrible."

Why isn't Not-Sheba bothered? Or is she in on this? Her head disappeared back up the chimney. Frank glanced back towards the mummy. The front of the mummy's case fell to the floor with a great knock; it shook and dust flew up. A moment later, out of one half of the case stepped a shrivelled, stained body, bound round with a few strips of dark cloth. The face was bony and shrunken, the bones pushing through the skin, the mouth clamped into an unsmiling grin. The movements were stiff and jerky and the head couldn't turn at the neck. Instead, the whole body inched around with a sound like the blade of a knife being scraped across a plate.

It's seen me, said Frank to himself – and it had. *I've seen this in a late night film on TV. Now, what happens next is ... it comes for me, because of the Pharaoh's curse on all grave-robbers. It's going to stagger towards me while the music goes eeee eeee eeee!* Frank whispered up the chimney, "It's coming for me, Not-Sheba. This is where it strangles me. I've seen it in the film."

The moment Frank said that, the mummy groaned. It was now only a few feet away and Frank could smell its sweet-musty body. A great, ghastly, meaty, sad groan.

"Did you say 'film'?" said the mummy.

"Yes, sir," said Frank.

"I knew it," said the mummy, "I knew it."

"What did you know, sir?" said Frank, playing for time before the moment when the mummy's fingers would reach out for his throat and squeeze the breath out of him and he would fall to the floor with a thud.

"You're the man for me," said the mummy.

"Yes, I know that as well, sir," said Frank. "This is where you strangle me before you climb back into the tomb. I've seen it."

"You've seen it? You've seen it? I knew it, you're my man."

The worksheet, Mr Butcher, Mrs Morrell waiting at the coach – all slipped from Frank's head. The end was coming. He didn't have to worry any more whether he was for the scrap heap, the dung heap or any old heap. He didn't have to

35

worry about this weird girl he was with. He'd be found stone dead, strangled, on the floor of Chiltern House next to the Mummy's Tomb; the Pharaoh's curse still working. Frank calmed himself for the end. He knew that as the mummy's hands closed round his throat, he would raise his own hands to the mummy's arms in an attempt to wrench them off him. But *the grip would be too strong. It would be the iron grip of Three Thousand Years of Fate.* The mummy's face jerked near, Frank could see each stained tooth right around the jaw. It was about to speak to him. *Yes,* Frank thought, *this is where it screams,* "THE PHARAOH'S CURSE LIVES ON!!!"

"Can you get me a part?" it said.

"What?" said Frank.

"Can you get me a part?" it said again.

"A part of what?" said Frank.

"A part in the film," it said.

"I don't know," said Frank. This bit wasn't in the film he knew. The mummy in the film he watched that night didn't talk *about* a film when it was actually *in* a film.

"I want to be the mummy in the film," said

the mummy. "I want the part. Believe me, I can act. I know I look a bit stiff, but that'd be right for the part wouldn't it? Please . . . please."

"I don't make films," said Frank. "I mean, I'm sure you'd be great but I'm just a kid . . . I don't . . ."

"Don't try and be funny with me. Don't try and be funny, kid."

"I never try to be funny, sir," said Frank, "it just comes out that way sometimes."

"I mean business," said the mummy. "For years and years, I've been locked up in there listening to people walking past laughing at me, talking about the great mummy films I remind them of: 'The Curse of the Mummy's Tomb', 'The Mummy Rises Again', 'The Mummy's Shroud'. I listen and I remember. I remember and I listen. And now that I'm finally out, I want a bit of the action. I suppose it's Tutankhamun who gets all the parts, isn't it? He always did have more fun than me. Well, now it's my turn. My break. And you, kid, you are going to put me in your movie or you're finished."

Frank could see it wasn't going to be much

use trying to explain to the mummy that he didn't really make films. In fact, it wasn't going to be much use trying to explain anything or say anything to the mummy.

"I want the fame. I want the glory!" It was shouting now. "I want to be the one who steps up on that stage, with the whole world watching, to collect my Oscar. I want to be the one to make the witty speech and collect my little Oscar statue. I want to be given it by someone the whole world knows, like Madonna or Adolf Hitler."

"I don't think Adolf Hitler is alive any more," said Frank.

"Well, Cleopatra then," said the mummy.

"Right," said Frank. *Best not to argue, he thought.*

"You got it," said the mummy. "So get me the part, OK?"

"Er – OK," said Frank. *Now what have I let myself in for? he thought. First I get myself stuck with some hopeless hunt for someone's name, and now I'm supposed to be a film director making horror films.*

"Now we're talking business," said the mummy.

"Yep," said Frank. "What shall I call you, then?"

"Charlie," said the mummy. "Wasn't he a great man in movies? Charlie Chappie? Charlie Chappin? Or something?"

"Yes," said Frank, "he was. He was brilliant." And just to test the mummy, he said, "You look like him as well."

"I thought so," said the mummy.

Not-Sheba put her head down the chimney. "Can I be in the film as well?"

"Oh yes, of course," said Frank, amazing himself at the way he was talking.

"Who's this?" said Charlie the mummy.

"Not-Sheba," said Frank.

"Not the Queen of Not-Sheba?" said Charlie, "from that great movie, 'Solomon and Not-Sheba' starring Yul Brynner, directed by King Vidor?"

Frank glanced at Not-Sheba to see how she would take this, but she was too busy staring at Charlie's horrible face. Then suddenly she realised who it was: the mummy. They had called out to each other on occasions on long, lonely winter nights but she had no idea that he looked like this. And of course, he didn't know that her name was Not-Sheba. Not Not-Sheba. Now she was getting confused herself. Charlie didn't seem too bothered to know that she was the girl in the picture who had talked to him sometimes and he didn't wait for the answer to his question either.

"That's great. That's great," he said. "What a line-up. Not-Sheba and Charlie Chappin the mummy. This is going to be a great movie."

"FRANK!" A man's loud voice shouted out, followed by a thudding, clanking noise.

"Oh no, it's Mr Butcher," said Frank, "and I haven't done anything for my worksheet. Quick, give it back to me, Not-Sheba!"

"Nope," said Not-Sheba. "We haven't got any-where towards finding my name yet."

Frank glanced at Charlie, wondering if he was trying to follow this conversation. He hadn't heard. He was too busy rehearsing 'The Mum-my Rises Again' by rising again and again all over the place.

Then Mr Butcher strode into the room. *Well,*

it looks like Mr Butcher except he isn't wearing his usual brown jacket and black trousers. Is that him, Mr Butcher himself, in a suit of armour with a sword in his hand? "FRANK!" bellowed the man in a familiar voice, and waved the sword.

"I know what this means," said Not-Sheba, "quick, let's run for it." And she dropped herself down from the chimney.

Charlie, the mummy, looked round and stared. He seemed to know too. "Oh no," he said.

"I'll follow you two," said Frank as Not-Sheba and Charlie started running off. The clanking Mr Butcher person, sword in hand, strode after them.

Start at the Beginning

"In the cupboard," said Not-Sheba, "he can't undo the latch."

In went Not-Sheba first, followed by Charlie and then Frank. The three of them stood close together in the dark. The smell coming from Charlie was terrible. He smelt like something that had been lying under a stone which had been lying under a dog for many, many years.

The sound of the Mr Butcher person in the suit of armour was getting closer. Crunk, cronk, crunk, cronk, crunk, cronk.

"How do you know him? Is he on show here too?" said Frank.

"We don't just know him," said Not-Sheba,

"he's part of the furniture. He's here, there and everywhere."

It wasn't an answer to his question but Frank was learning that there were going to be many more questions than answers just now.

"This will make a great scene in the movie," said Charlie. "You could have a completely dark screen and with just us whispering."

"I'm not whispering," said Not-Sheba.

"Who have you got in mind for cameraman?" said Charlie.

Frank felt helpless. Well, he was helpless, stuck in a cupboard with an ancient Egyptian mummy, an old-fashioned girl who had taken his worksheet off him and a knight-in-armour cronking and crunking outside.

"I know you're there," said the knight.

"Yeah, but there's nothing you can do about it, is there?" said Not-Sheba, because you've got those stupid metal gloves on."

"Come on. Out you come and get back to where you belong."

"Never," said Not-Sheba. "I'm on my way to finding out my real name. I'm not going back to where you say I belong. I'm going back to where I say I belong."

"And I'm going to be a STAR!" shouted Charlie.

Frank couldn't think what he was doing, so he said, "And I'm in the cupboard," which everyone knew anyway.

"Yes," said the knight, "And what are you doing in there, Frank?"

"How does he know your name?" said Not-Sheba.

"He's my head teacher."

"Your head teacher? Him? He's not your head teacher."

"I know he's not dressed like my head teacher but I'm pretty sure it is him. Now shhhh. I'd better talk to him: I'm doing my worksheet, sir," said Frank.

"In a cupboard?"

"Yessir, they're helping me. Erm – I'm working on the question about the er . . . quick, Not-Sheba, pass me the worksheet."

"There's not much point in passing it to you – you won't be able to read it in the dark,"

Not-Sheba said.

"What question am I doing, though?" said Frank.

"I don't know," she said, "I haven't read it."

"Well?" said Mr Butcher, "what question ARE you working on?"

"I'm working on the question about – er . . ."

"The mummy," whispered Not-Sheba.

"The mummy," said Frank.

"I would agree to appear on chat shows and breakfast television," said Charlie.

"Good," said Mr Butcher. "Make sure you get your facts right, and make sure you start at the very beginning."

"He wouldn't start at the end, would he?" said Not-Sheba, "Because that wouldn't be the beginning would it? Mind you, wherever you start is the beginning isn't it, or are you too stupid to understand that?"

Frank was shocked she was talking to Mr Butcher like that, especially as he had a sword in his hand. If it was Mr Butcher. Mr Butcher started growling. "If I get my hands on you, my girl, there'll be trouble. You'll be back on that picture quicker than it takes you to write your name."

How does he know Not-Sheba? How does Not-Sheba know Mr Butcher? Frank had a feeling he didn't know anything about anything.

"Oh, jump in the lake and get your bum rusty," said Not-Sheba.

"That wasn't me that said that, sir," said Frank.

"Oh, it was you, Frank then, was it?" said Mr Butcher.

Frank felt helpless again. Not-Sheba giggled. "It will all go down on your report, son, I can tell you," said Mr Butcher.

There was a bit more crunking and they heard Mr Butcher's armour footsteps pacing off. Not-Sheba opened the door. They were in a corridor.

"Look," said Frank, "I really can't hang about here with you two anymore. It's been really nice being with you and thanks for–"

Not-Sheba grabbed Frank from one side, Charlie from the other.

"Not so fast," said Charlie in an American voice. "You try and cross the state line I'll call the bureau. Just zip your lips, smiler."

"That's right," said Not-Sheba, enjoying all

this, "you're going to help me or I'll eat your worksheet."

"OK OK OK," said Frank, and he tried thinking fast about how he could help all three of them: the two of them and himself all at the same time. He tried thinking fast but nothing happened. So he went back to thinking slowly. "I've got it," he said, "We need to start at the beginning, don't we?"

"Oh aren't you a clever boy!" said Not-Sheba. "We've just had to put up with that sort of garbage from old Rusty-bum."

"No, no," said Frank, "the beginning of this place. We can only find out your name by starting at the beginning of this place, Chiltern Wotsit . . . finding out where you came from, how you got here. We've got to get back to the beginning. How it got to be here." Thinking to himself: *And then I can get the stuff I need to answer the questions.*

Charlie interrupted in a cockney gangster voice – "And what's my cut on this job, John? Or are you fellas planning to leave me in the cold while I dig me cabbages?"

"Right," said Frank, "what we need to do is find good, find good . . ."

"Locations," said Charlie. "Now we're beginning to get a bit of energy flowing on this project. Good locations speak to you. They tell you good shots, good angles. A good location is a story in itself. This is cinema," he said, and held out his hand like someone being interviewed coming up with a great thought, "This is cinema."

Not-Sheba and Charlie were no longer gripping Frank. "So what we need to do now," said Frank, "is find the oldest part of this place. The oldest part will be the beginning part."

"And ancient voices will speak to us," said Charlie.

He is very difficult, thought Frank.

"And when we get there," said Frank, talking as slowly as he thought, "we ask a few questions. Do you two know where we go?"

"The chapel," said Not-Sheba.

"My mummy case," said Charlie.

"Let's try the chapel," said Frank, feeling sick at the thought of being stuck inside Charlie's mummy case for more than one and a half seconds. But Charlie wasn't listening. The word 'old' had obviously gripped him, or perhaps it was the word 'chapel' and Charlie would soon be thinking of one of those Shakespeare films they'd had to see a few months ago. Frank was right. In a moment, Charlie was strutting about as if he was on stage and reciting:

"Methinks 'tis good we sally forth

So bright and early on Saint Patrick's day . . ."

"It's not Saint Patrick's day, is it?" said Frank.

"Herein do I imitate the sun

Who doth allow . . .

er . . . er . . . CUT. Cut it," said Charlie, interrupting his flow of words. "Learn your lines, dammit, learn your lines, Charlie. Break for lunch."

"Maybe you're an Ancient Egyptian," said Frank to Not-Sheba.

"Let's go to the chapel," said Not-Sheba.

The Festival of Fools

The chapel was cold and quiet. You could almost see the silence.

"This is the chapel," whispered Not-Sheba.

"Why are you whispering?" whispered Frank.

"I'm not whispering," whispered Charlie.

"I wasn't talking to you," whispered Frank.

"Why not?" whispered Charlie, "don't you like me any more?"

"Do you think I came from here?" whispered Not-Sheba.

There was a loud whoop. It wasn't a scream, and it wasn't a yell. It was a wild, happy, loopy whoop.

They looked round. There was nothing and nobody.

"Grave-robber," said Charlie. "That's what grave robbers do."

"What are grave-robbers?" asked Frank.

"People who rob graves," said Charlie not very helpfully.

There was another whoop.

"I was grave-robbed," said Charlie in a rather grand and proud voice. He went on, "grave-robbed many, many times. First time wasn't long after they put me in my pyramid. Last time was when Lord Chiltern brought me here. They all whooped. Got into the tomb, whooped, picked something up and left. They liked gold stuff mostly. By the time Lord Chiltern got there, there was only me and the cat left. Good enough for him: he whooped, picked me up and left like the rest of them. Mind you, if I'd stayed there, I'd never have got into films, would I? When I'm a star..."

"I wonder if they whooped when they found me?" said Not-Sheba.

Frank was thinking he didn't much like whooping, especially in this cold, silent place.

Then there came a great chorus of whooping.

51

It seemed to be coming from up above. They looked up. On the chapel walls, high up, sitting between each window, each one on a kind of stone plate, was a head, also made of stone. No body, just a head. There were about twenty of them, each pulling a weird face: some grinning, some sticking their tongues out, some pulling their lips apart with their fingers. They were all whooping. Then, one by one, they flew off their perches high up on the walls and floated down towards Frank and his friends. Even when they started flying, they didn't have any bodies below, yet they behaved as if they did have them and the heads floated in the air at head-height.

"It's Christmas again," screamed one of them at Frank. Frank looked at his watch.

"No, actually it's 23rd March."

They ignored him. "It's the Festival of Fools!" More whooping.

The three visitors found themselves being caught by the arms and whirled around and around. The heads grinned and cackled and a rush of music filled the chapel. It was wild, piping music with a rhythm that made them dance.

Not the kind of dancing the girls do in my class, Frank thought, *more a wild, flinging-yourself-around dance.* All the heads danced and danced round and round the chapel, up and down the aisles and in and out the pews.

Soon the chapel was ablaze with colour because the heads grabbed green and yellow and red scarves and ribbons. Where their hands and ankles would have been, they had tied coloured handkerchiefs and bunches of bells. As they danced, the colours streamed out and the bells shook and tinkled. Frank, Not-Sheba and Charlie were soon decked out as well. One of the heads pulled out a mad-looking hobby-horse, decked it in coloured streamers, and soon it was capering about as if it had a life of its own. And all the time, the piping piped, drums drummed, and the heads whooped.

Food and drink appeared from out of cubby holes in the wall, from out of little doorways: cakes, meat-pies, chicken, bottles of wine, roast pork, and the heads fed themselves with their invisible arms and called on Not-Sheba, Frank and Charlie to join in. Frank made for the cake,

Not-Sheba for the meat pies and Charlie for the wine. Round and round went the dancing heads, their scarves and hankies weaving in and out. Some were singing too. The song sounded to Frank like it was round-and-round as well:

"A round, a round, a roundelay

A round, a round, a roundelay."

Frank joined in with a cake in his hand, yellow hankies tied to his wrists, jingling bells tied round his knees, and over there, across the chapel weaving in and out of the heads and their streamers were Not-Sheba and Charlie. They were flinging themselves about like the heads and the hobbyhorse were. The air was full of the smell of the food, the sound of the music, the yellows and greens and reds of the clothes and the patchy, shaky light of the candles.

Not-Sheba had a mad, reckless look on her face, as it appeared and disappeared between the laughing and shouting heads. Charlie was wild. He was shaking his head and bandages as if he was trying to say no a thousand times in a minute. He was jumping up and down and whooping like a bunch of grave-robbers. Frank felt light and dizzy.

Then one of the heads shouted: "Clothes off!" And there was a great roar and outburst of laughter; the men-heads looked at the women-heads; there were screams and giggles and winks and nods all round. On went the dance, whirring and whirling round.

"Come on you two," shouted a woman-head, pulling at Frank's trousers.

"It's all right for you," said Frank, "you're invisible."

"Off, off, off, off, off," shouted the heads.

Not-Sheba and Frank clung to their clothes but Charlie loved it. Off came the old stained cloth bandages and soon he was dancing around naked, his shrivelled, skinny brown body snaking in and out of the pews. The heads loved it too, and whooped and whirred about even more.

"Off, off, off," the heads shouted at Not-Sheba and Frank. Frank felt sick with embarrassment. Not-Sheba looked terrified and held on to her clothes. Invisible hands pulled at them; heads grinned and sang all around them. The yellows and greens waved and fluttered. Charlie was in a trance, wobbling and whooping more than anybody; a red scarf flew out behind him as he wobbled. Then another call went up: "The bishop, the bishop, the bishop!"

Saved, thought Frank, the bishop must be coming. He won't let them rip my trousers off. Bishops are serious men in big gowns and cloak-things who do church services on Sunday on the telly. He'll tell them to stop all this stuff.

"The boy, the boy!" shouted the heads, "He's our bishop."

Frank looked round for a boy-bishop, but just as he did so, he felt himself lifted off his feet. Someone threw a disgusting, dirty, smelly sheet round his shoulders. He was being carried round the chapel and from where he sat, he could look down at the heads' faces grinning and cackling up at him.

The music changed. *This sounds more like hymns,* he thought, but Frank could hear there were rude words. He tried to catch exactly what they were but just as it got to the rude bit, everyone roared and laughed and he missed it. One he made out was something to do with 'loving God with all my heart . . . something something something makes me –' and everyone screamed out laughing. Charlie was over the moon. This was the best time he'd had since . . . well, in about three thousand years. Frank was carried around on invisible shoulders, up and down the aisles wrapped in the disgusting sheet. At his side, two of the heads had a kind of ornamental basket on the end of a chain.

"Yes, the censer, the censer," the heads shouted, and to Frank's amazement, he saw them stuffing what looked very much like horse dung into the basket. Then, even more amazingly, they set light to it and then walked up and down the aisles near Frank whirling the little ornamental basket full of burning horse dung round and round on the end of the chain.

A new call went up: "The service, the service," and Frank found himself lowered down in front of the altar. "A sermon, a sermon," the heads shouted at Frank.

The shout got taken up, the music played wildly again. "A sermon, a sermon, a sermon," they called to Frank.

"What's a sermon?" shouted Frank back at them.

"Tell us how bad we've been, bishop, tell us what to do, bishop," they shouted.

Frank saw in his mind's eye the bishop on telly talking to the people. He was quite good at voices and he found himself saying: "When almighty Hubbly-Bubbly spoke unto Jelly-belly . . ."

The heads loved it. They whooped like mad.

Frank went on: ". . . Hubbly-Bubbly did say: 'Go forth,' but Jelly-Belly spoke unto almighty Hubbly-Bubbly: 'Go fourth? Go fourth? I don't want to go fourth, I want to go first or second.'" The heads cheered. The music whirled. "More, bishop! More, bishop!" and they swung the censer round and round so that the smell of the burning horse dung filled the chapel.

Then came the big surprise.

The chapel door banged open. The wind blew the candles; some spluttered, others blew out. There, in the doorway, stood the suit of armour again: the helmet shut tight, the sword aloft. The music stopped. No one moved. A voice boomed out from inside the armour: "Enough!"

It was that Mr Butcher person in armour again. He was furious. Frank didn't even know where the worksheet was. He certainly wasn't working on it. He tried to shrink out of sight under his dirty sheet. Then something happened. Out of the corner of his eye, he noticed some kind of movement. What was it?

It was a stone body, lying in an alcove. It was moving.

Mr Butcher strode down the aisle towards Frank. *But what is the body doing and who is it?* Frank could see that it was a monk and it slid noiselessly out from its alcove and joined Mr Butcher next to Frank. There they stood, Frank, Mr Butcher in his armour, and the stone monk, all looking at the heads. The bright colours were motionless, though Charlie was still shaking about, stark-naked. Not-Sheba folded her arms and watched.

Mr Butcher-in-armour turned to the stone monk. He seemed to know him. "Father Abbot, are they causing trouble again?"

Father Abbott? Abbott? That's a sort of boss of the monks, isn't it?

"Yes, Sir William, they are."

"You know, you can always send the ring leaders to me," Mr Butcher-in-armour said.

"Of course," said Father Abbot.

"We was only mucking about a bit," said one of the heads.

"Yeah, and why not?" said another. "We work all year round for that pot-bellied monk, so why shouldn't we have a bit of a romp at Christmas?"

Frank was trying to figure out who these heads were. *People who work in the fields? And then they sleep up there on those stone plates. That seemed odd but possible. Or was it possible but odd?*

"Enough," shouted Mr Butcher-in-armour, "no one asked you to speak out of turn."

"You haven't looked in that box behind you, sir," said another head. Father Abbot, the monk, looked uneasy.

"We're not talking about boxes," said Mr Butcher, "we're talking about your behaviour. Frank, what do you think you're doing dressed up in that dirty bit of cloth? What is it anyway?"

"It's my worksheet," said Frank.

"Look in the box, sir," said one of the heads.

Charlie had stopped shaking and now stood next to Not-Sheba. "Gee, I so love old musicals. Have you seen 'Jesus Christ Super Star?' 'Hello Dolly'? 'Mary Poppins'?" Not-Sheba shook her head. "'Oklahoma'? 'Starlight Express'? 'Joseph and his Technicolour Dreamcoat'?" Not-Sheba shook her head to all three. "I'll have a word with Frank," said Charlie, "maybe we'll do a musical instead of a horror film. What do you think?"

"All I know, Charlie," said Not-Sheba, "is that I don't think I'm much to do with this lot. I'm not going to find my name here."

"Open the box," the heads shouted.

Mr Butcher-in-armour seemed to hesitate and then moved back towards a great wooden chest. It was locked. "Father Abbot, do you have the key?"

The stone monk pulled out a key from under his cloak. Mr Butcher opened the box. Inside were golden crosses, jewelled cups and chalices, ornamental silver swords, gold cloth, brooches, buckles, gold and silver candlesticks. The box was piled high with it. Everyone crowded round, gasping and oohing.

"That's a lot of lost property for one week, Father Abbot," said Mr Butcher.

Sometimes he seems more like Mr Butcher than Mr Butcher-in-armour.

The heads moved in closer.

Charlie called out from the back, "Sing – sing a chorus number, you know:

'Jesus Christ, Superstar

Who are you? Who do you think you are?'"

"Well, Father Abbot," said Mr Butcher-in-armour, "I have a letter here from the King. He says, 'dum de dum de dum – er anything found in old boxes . . . blank blank blank blank, belongs to me, so, Sir William Butcher, you are called upon dah de dah de dah de dah to grab it – (or words to that effect). All the best, Henry.'"

"But – but all this belongs to the Monastery," said Father Abbot, "It belongs to God."

"No, no, no!" shouted Charlie, "not a musical. Forget that. Music Hall, good old time Music Hall. You know the sort of thing:

'I'm Henery the Eighth I am, I am

Henery the Eighth I am

I got married to the widow next door

She's been —'"

"For goodness sake, Charlie, put some clothes on and shut up," said Not-Sheba.

"Hang on, Abbot," shouted the heads, "that gold's ours. "

Mr Butcher-in-armour raised his sword and cut through the air with a swish. The heads fell back.

"Barn-loads of wheat and barley we harvested for him, and barn-loads were sold off to buy all that gold stuff, while we've gone hungry." The sword swished again.

"Did you see 'Camelot'?" said Charlie to Not-Sheba. "Lovely songs, lovely costumes."

Father Abbot was crouching in the corner crying.

"Frank!" bellowed Mr Butcher.

"Oh no, he's noticed me again" said Frank.

"Question 4 on the worksheet." *So is it Mr Butcher?*

Frank pretended to look very closely at the

dirty sheet round his shoulders.

"Yessir!" said Frank.

"Not 'Yessir'," said Mr Butcher, "the answer, son, the answer."

"What's the question again, sir?"

"Question 4 – Who received the Chapel and several thousand acres of land belonging to the monastery as reward for his services to the king?"

Charlie sung out, 'I'm her eighth old man called Henery – I'm Henery the –'" Not-Sheba covered his mouth.

Frank looked blankly into the far distance. One of the heads stared back and shouted: "Sir William Butcher, the first Lord Chiltern."

Ahh, Butcher. Butcher, the same name.

"Yessir," said Frank, "Sir William Butcher, the first Lord Chiltern."

"Good, son, good. Fill it in on the worksheet and for goodness sake," said the man in armour sounding distinctly like the Mr Butcher he knew, prodding Frank with the end of his sword, "get a move on, lad."

At that, Mr Butcher-in-armour flicked his

fingers at a few of the heads and pointed at the box. Turning to Father Abbot, he said, "The King has wars to fight, wives to find, feasts to eat, you know. On to London, you lot." The invisible arms lifted the box, Mr Butcher-in-armour strode off through the chapel door, followed by the heads carrying the box.

Other heads mumbled and grumbled their way back to their perches between the windows, talking to each other with: "Huh! For 'services to the King'! All William Butcher did was chuck the pot-bellied abbot out and supply his own pot-belly instead. Didn't make no difference to us. Nice for old Butcher though. He got a lordship out of it. Lord Chiltern now, wasn't he? Just from digging a sword into the abbot's ribs, relieving him of his gold and handing it over to King Harry. Nice for some, eh?"

Father Abbot went back to his dark alcove in the wall still crying.

Frank, Not-Sheba and Charlie looked at each other . . .

Well, at least we've started at the beginning of this place, like I said we should, thought Frank.

So Lovely Here

…but not for long.

A large, sleek dog, wearing a black cloak and a gold collar, paced neatly into the chapel, one paw after another landing on the ground with a graceful phut. "If you're with the party," it said in a very haughty voice, "would you be so kind as to keep UP!"

At last, thought Frank, this dog can take me to the rest of my class, and I'll be able to get on with my work.

Charlie, Not-Sheba and Frank followed the Dog down the corridor into another huge, high, light room. There they joined a group of people who were obviously visitors to Chiltern House. It was obvious but for one thing: they were all kneeling.

The Dog spoke: "The ceiling is decorated in gold leaf with Lanscroon's depiction of the five daughters."

A little whisper of, "Oh yes, lovely," came from the people kneeling on the floor. There were almost twenty of them, all ages, men and women, all dressed in their going-out, must-look-good clothes.

"Notice the oyster walnut side-table and the one beneath the window with floral marquetry picked out in blue-green stained ivory." The group of people hurried across, still on their knees, to see the table. They pressed themselves against the blue cord and oohed and aahed some more.

"They lived with such style," whispered one man to a woman next to him.

"The wall clock is by Tompion," said the Dog and swept out. The group hurried after on their knees, whispering and sighing to each other.

"Such a wonderful time to have lived through," said the woman back to the man.

Frank, Charlie and Not-Sheba followed too.

"The Pomegranate Room," said the Dog, "so

called because of its elaborate plasterwork frieze of pomegranates. The ormolu six-branch candelabra is by Boulton. The green-and-white dinner service with the family crest is of Marseille faience."

"What's all this about?" said Frank who hadn't understood a word of what the Dog had been saying.

"It's the stuff," said Not-Sheba.

"I see," said Frank.

"Where did you get it from?" said Charlie to Frank.

"Get it?"

"It'll look great. It reminds me of when Barbara Streisand dances down that flight of stairs in 'Hello Dolly'. I can do that you know. I could be the Barbara Streisand of the pyramids."

"Yes, you could," said Frank who had never seen 'Hello Dolly'. He wondered if it was a film about dolls who keep meeting and saying "Hello, Dolly!" to each other. He thought he'd better start listening to the Dog in case he could pick up some answers to the worksheet. Good idea – if only he understood a word of what the

Dog was saying.

"Excuse me," said one of the men kneeling in front of an old chair. "How much would a piece like that be worth?"

"Priceless," said the Dog. "Priceless. It was designed by the greatest interior designer of the day – or perhaps ever – working two hundred years ago. The chair matches the ceiling, the fireplaces, the door handles and even the tassels on the curtains. As part of the total décor it is priceless. Separated from here, it would be a . . . tragedy." The Dog's voice trembled as it said 'tragedy', as if its mother had just died.

Charlie imitated it quietly in a corner on his own: "Priceless, priceless, tragedy, tragedy."

All the kneeling people looked at the old chair and they nodded their heads towards it, rather as if they were praying, and they too, all said "Priceless, priceless, tragedy, tragedy."

"I think it's wonderful it's still in the Chiltern family," whispered one of the kneelers.

The Dog swept across the room and came to a halt in front of a massive picture. "The temples and monuments that you see in the background you may visit in the grounds," it said. "They were built by Henry Butcher, later to become Lord Admiral Chiltern, after his spectacular voyage around the world in 1745, a journey which . . . how shall I say? . . . enormously enriched him."

Not that name again?

Frank looked out of the window and saw the very same temples and monuments that were in the picture and he looked back at the Admiral. He was quite small. "Hmm," said Frank, "he's not exactly enormous enough to have built all those by himself. Amazing."

Not-Sheba looked at Frank. "*He* didn't, you fool. There was a gang of masons on that lot for over a year. I remember them being here."

"But the Dog just said —"

Charlie interrupted. "Frank, you see that temple?"

"Yep."

"Do you remember when Christopher Lee did 'Dracula Rises Again' he burst out of his grave at midnight, pulling the stake out of his chest?"

"I don't actually remember that one, but go on."

"I could lug my mummy case out there and we could get a similar effect with me."

"Good idea, Charlie," said Frank.

By now, the Dog had led the kneeling group off to another room. They carried on whispering excitedly and politely to each other.

"So lovely here."

"What a shame they don't still live here."

"What does he do, the present Lord Chiltern?"

"Is there one?"

"Not sure, darling."

By the time Frank and the others had caught up with the Dog, it was talking again. It had speeded up and was beginning to gabble breathlessly.

". . . splendid pair of Ch'ien Lung goose tureens . . . mounted on Dutch silver bases . . . dignified and serene . . . magnificent ebony cabinet . . . flowered damask curtains . . . superb collection of weapons and other military mementos . . ."

The kneelers speeded up as well and were bowing and nodding and whispering like mad to keep up with the Dog. "Marvellous," (nod, nod, bow), "beautiful", (bow, nod, bow), "wonderful", (bow, nod, nod). The whole thing seemed to get faster and faster – "pure gold cornerpieces . . . inlaid ivory panels . . ." (bow, nod, nod), "lovely", "mother of pearl façade" (nod, nod), "Oooooh" – until the Dog suddenly flung open some doors at the end of the room and pointed out to the far, far distance. It gabbled towards a triumphal climax:

". . . the whole vista you see before you, designed and landscaped by Jeremiah Green with unforgettable grandeur." It stopped. The kneelers gasped and then clapped politely and, then, running off on their knees as fast as they could go, they wobbled off out of the door, their lips full of 'thank yous' and 'delightfuls' and 'so nices'. The Dog watched until they were all gone, scurrying along the avenue of trees, round the fountains and out towards the temple and the monuments. It closed the doors, turned back into the room, and under its breath it muttered: "The public! Ugh! Frightful, absolutely frightful." It shuddered as if to shake off a foul smell or some drips of invisible and revolting slime.

Then it noticed Frank and his companions. "Do you three have a permit?" it said.

Charlie moved closer. "Listen, Dog," he said, "I am three thousand years old. After so many years on this earth I don't expect to be bossed about by somebody's little dog."

"What about the other two?" it said haughtily.

"Listen, Dog," said Charlie again, "Chiltern House is about to achieve world-wide fame. It is to be the location of an earth-shattering blockbuster of a moving picture. You are looking, Dog, at three people vital to its success."

The dog humphed, turned on its heels and paced off.

"Nerd!" said Charlie, "Every time it gets to me on its rounds it says that I was a pharaoh. Pharaoh, my eye! I was a priest, not a pharaoh."

"It's all right for *you*! It doesn't even *see* me," said Not-Sheba.

"Wait a minute," said Charlie in his smooth-talking Hollywood nice-guy voice, a mix between Cary Grant and George Clooney. "So you're the girl I spoke to last night?"

"Well," said Not-Sheba, sounding offended that it had taken Charlie this long to figure out who she was, "yes, we have sometimes talked to each other, but it wasn't last night. And when we talked, I thought you were nicer than this."

"You know that gold that Mr Butcher-in-armour said he was taking off to the King, you know, in that chest?" said Frank.

"Yes," said Not-Sheba.

"I bet he kept some of it."

"What makes you think that?"

"I don't know," said Frank, looking round at the huge pictures and carpets and everything else that the Dog had pointed out. "I don't know yet."

"You don't know very much, do you?" said Not-Sheba. Frank felt jumpy. She was getting nearer, looking determined and cross. "You said you'd help me," she said, "and then I was going to help you. So far you're getting nowhere.

Nowhere at all. If this goes on much longer I'm going to rip your silly little worksheet into tiny little bits, and then you can take the pile of all the scraps and shreds left over and hand them back to your Head Teacher fellow, and then see what'll happen to you."

Frank felt terrible. She seemed to know that coming face to face with Mr Butcher could be a pretty ghastly business.

"Don't worry," said Charlie, comforting him, "once we crack on with this movie, she won't be anywhere near so cross. See, the chick's gone cold on me too."

"I am not a chick, OK?"

"How's the script coming on?" said Charlie to Frank.

Frank felt more terrible.

One moment these two seemed to be his friends and next they were really quite scary. He looked about him. Any moment now, Mr Butcher or Mr Butcher-in-armour – or perhaps this Admiral Butcher in some kind of sailor's outfit – would probably turn up again. He looked round some more and found himself staring at yet another massive picture on the wall. It was a sea-battle between some very old ships. Cannons were firing. He thought quickly for the first time in ages and said to Charlie: "We could always do a kind of sea-adventure film, 'Mutiny on the Bounty', 'Pirates of the Caribbean' – that sort of thing." Charlie seemed interested.

Not-Sheba thought for a moment. "Maybe I come from the sea," she said.

Frank breathed in a quick little breath, thinking – *that was a good line to take, perhaps that'll keep them happy for a bit.*

Not-Sheba and Charlie walked off towards the sea-battle picture, getting quite close up to it. Frank looked all around him, wondering if he could slip away while they weren't looking. Yes, he could. But that was no good unless he could get his worksheet off Not-Sheba. *And how am I going to do that?*

He plotted.

Chapter 8

Where is India?

Charlie and Not-Sheba went on and on looking at the sea-battle, almost as if they were trying to climb into it. Frank stood back from them. Charlie was getting excited.

"I could be lying on the deck of the ship in my mummy case. The ship has been commandeered by Admiral Lord Chiltern to take me back to England from Egypt with the treasure from my tomb. Suddenly a pirate ship is spotted to the west. All the hands on deck! We hoist the tops'l and pick up speed, but the pirate ship is quicker and hoves to. Soon she is alongside. We see their faces as they hurl the grappling iron and we hear the cry: "Board her! Board her!" and the pirates leap aboard.

"As they clamber on deck, they seize our sailors and hold them with knives to their throats. Two of them rush below and find the treasure and come up on deck, their hands full of jewels and gold ornaments. Just as they are rejoicing over their find, there comes a loud creaking, cracking noise, and I rise from my case . . . Aaaaaaaaaagh! The curse of the Pharaoh's gold! I walk stiffly towards the nearest pirate. He shoots, but the bullet just bounces off me. I reach him. I take hold of him with my skinny, bony hands and bit by bit, step by step, I crush him with the grip of three thousand years of vengeance."

Charlie stopped, breathless and exultant. Not-Sheba looked curious.

"Why would you crush the pirate, when it was Admiral Lord Chiltern who nicked the Pharaoh's gold in the first place?"

"Because Admiral Lord Chiltern is a goody. The goodies never get done in. Don't you know anything?"

Frank could see his worksheet just poking out of the back of Not-Sheba's dress. If he got near enough, he could whip it out and do a run for it.

"What do you think, Frank?" said Charlie, pointing back at the sea-battle, "Could we do that?" Could we shoot that one?"

"Yes," said Frank trying to look serious. "Yes, it sounds like a great idea."

Charlie looked back at the sea-battle, his eyes gleaming. Frank got nearer to the worksheet; one more reach and he'd be there. He began to reach out his arm when a voice spoke out: "Why are you doing that?"

Charlie and Frank spoke at the same time. Charlie said, "I'm just helping out with the script." Frank said, "I was just stretching my arm."

They looked round. There was a little laugh and then a giggle.

"I surprised you, huh?"

"Who said that?" said Charlie.

"Is the woman with you a princess?" said the voice.

Not-Sheba looked surprised and a little pleased. "Well, I'm not a woman," she said modestly, "but I suppose I could be a princess."

"What's your name?"

"I don't know," said Not-Sheba, "but who are you? And *where* are you?"

"I'm over here, on the priceless, priceless white-and-gilt sideboard table, bearing the mask of Hercules," said the voice imitating the dog in black, and then burst out giggling again.

Frank had lost his chance and so all three of them walked across to the table. There stood a funny-looking figure a bit like a monkey, made of ivory. "I'm Hanuman. Clever, clever, clever, clever chief of the monkeys – you can call me god of the monkeys if you like – and I need your help."

Frank felt tired, very, very, very, very, very tired. *Not again. Not somebody else asking for help?* He, Frank, was the only one round here needing help – and the help he needed most of all was how to get away from all these weird people with so many weird things to say.

"I have to find a beautiful princess," said Hanuman. "Of course, we would all like to find a beautiful princess but –"

"Speak for yourself," said Not-Sheba. "I might want to find a beautiful prince."

"I was going to say," said Hanuman, "I'm not looking for myself. I'm doing someone a favour, but I've got blown off course."

"Me too," said Frank glumly.

"I've landed up here, thousands of miles from where I should be," said Hanuman.

"Me too," said Charlie, "but it's OK for me, I'd never have got on in films if I'd stayed in my own country. Where are you from?"

"India," said Hanuman.

"Bollywood," said Charlie. "I thought so. Cool."

"Maybe you're Indian," said Frank to Not-Sheba, hoping for a quick end to this whole business.

"She's not," said Hanuman, squashing that one as quickly as it was suggested.

"How did you get here then?" Charlie asked Hanuman. "Are you part of the whole new Asian thing happening over here now?"

"Well, you see that picture you've been look-ing at?" said Hanuman. "You didn't get the story quite right. Admiral Lord Chiltern *was* the pirate. Not that he called himself that. Not that anyone called him that. He was an admiral and no one ever calls an admiral a pirate. Except me." He giggled again. Frank felt his eyes wobble. "You see," said Hanuman, " I was on board a Portuguese ship loaded down with Indian treasure and Admiral Lord Chiltern got his sailors to grab the lot and bring it back here. Call me a fibber, but I'd say that's what pirates do, isn't it? I'm worth thousands of pounds. Priceless, absolutely priceless." And he giggled some more.

A-thirsting for their Blood

"I think India must be in here," said Not-Sheba as if she was trying to remember a dream, and she pushed open the door. It was a long way from her painting and she was guessing where some of the voices came from. Once again there was a huge, high, light room with massive pictures on the wall, and chairs and tables and sofas all behind the same blue rope. On the tables and sideboards stood more figures and little statues.

Hanuman was whistling to himself. "My greatest leap ever. All the way back to India. Oh, I am wonderful. So clever, clever, clever."

"You know," said Charlie putting on some kind of horrible, smooth-man voice, "the movie people are thinking about the multicultural world we live in. Did you see 'Gladiator'?" He didn't wait for an answer. "The little fat guy who was Oliver Reed's assistant. You see, that's the sort of casting that goes on now. You could be a little fat guy like him. Though you're more what I'd just call 'little' rather than 'little fat'."

Frank looked round the room. This was India? *I thought India was a country. Maybe Mr Butcher was right. I don't deserve a place at the High School.* He caught sight of a CCTV camera rigged to a bracket on the wall.

"Welcome to India," said a man in the picture next to the door. He was tall, red-faced and he had a lot of clothes on. *Is this Mr Butcher again? It certainly looks like it.* Frank glanced at the little sign next to the picture. It said Lord Chiltern. His eye fell on little Hanuman.

"Are you Indian?" said this Lord Chiltern.

"Yes," said Hanuman.

"You can't move until you answer these questions: do you make shirts?" Hanuman scratched his head, thinking back hundreds of years.

"Yes, I do."

A monkey making shirts? Is Hanuman a shirt-maker?

Frank had a moment's clear thinking when he realised that in whatever world he was in just now, anyone could do anything, anything could be anybody. Some other kind of truth was going on.

"Where do you get the cotton to make the shirts with?" barked this Lord Chiltern-Butcherish person.

"I buy it from the farmer where I live."

"Well from now on," said Chiltern-Butcher, "you can't."

"Hey Charlie," said Frank, "see that camera?"

"Frank, baby, you're a genius. All this time you've had the cameras rigged up and you didn't tell me. So this is the location? Great. This is going to be a fabulous movie, Frank." Charlie looked around appreciating everything . . . "Wow, great, terrific, I like it . . ."

Hanuman seemed to be worrying about the shirts and muttering to himself: was Mr Butcher really saying that he couldn't buy cotton from the farmers any more? "But I will starve. I won't have cotton to make shirts, I won't have shirts to sell."

"No matter," said Mr Chiltern-Butcher, "this is the way that it is, now that I am in India."

"So now none of us will have shirts."

"Ah no, it's not like that," said Mr Chiltern-Butcher. "You see, I will be making the shirts in England and selling them to you."

"But you can't do that," said Hanuman excitedly, "because you haven't got any cotton."

"Oh yes I have. All the farmers in India who grow cotton now sell their cotton to me and me alone. Simple isn't it?"

"It sounds terrible," said Hanuman.

"Nice for me," said Mr Butcher, "because I will be able to make millions and millions of shirts and sell them all over the world and become very, very rich."

"Oh no you won't," said Hanuman bravely. "The farmers don't grow enough cotton for that."

"No, they don't now, but they will."

"But the farmers grow food on the fields so that we can live."

"Not any more they won't. Now they'll grow cotton."

"Oh no, I'm beaten," said Hanuman. "Now millions and millions of us starve, while you sell millions and millions of shirts."

"Are these video cameras?" said Charlie.

"I think so," said Frank.

"Then while we're about it, why not make a pop video? What are you into? R'n'b? Rap? Old-time Ballads? Retro, Sixties rock-stuff? Come on, man, let's do it. Let's do it."

"Hmm," said Frank.

Chiltern-Butcher and Hanuman were standing face to face.

"So do you understand everything now, little monkey?"

"Yes," said Hanuman, "I understand, but I don't like what I understand."

That's more than can be said for me, thought Frank.

"No matter," said Chiltern-Butcher. "If you understand, that's good enough, and you may pass."

Not-Sheba was wandering round the India room, looking at everything very closely. She wanted to find out if this was where she belonged. Perhaps she had been taken from India, she thought. Suddenly she came across a little statue of a beautiful woman and got talking.

"Hey Hanuman, man," said Charlie, "I've definitely got a part for you in this video."

"No, come over here, Hanuman," said Not-Sheba, "here's a princess. Weren't you looking for a princess? It says here, her name's Sita."

Hanuman shrieked, "Sita! Sita! That's it. That's her name. Sita! Sita! I have to give her this ring."

He rushed over to the statue. "Sita, Sita, here is the ring from – er – what's his name again? Oh no, I've forgotten his name."

Sita stirred and came to life. Her eyes turned slowly to the ring. A tear welled up in her eye as she looked at it.

"Take it," said Hanuman, "I've done it. I've performed my task. I've jumped – with these people's help – all the way back to India and given you the ring from er – whatsisname."

"From Rama," said Sita. "Thank you, Hanuman, but I have to tell you that this isn't India. I, too, was brought here by Lord Chiltern. My Rama was a beautiful ivory statue sitting next to me on the sideboard in a palace, thousands of miles away from here in the real India."

"Let's go," said Hanuman. "I can leap, I can fly."

"No, no, Hanuman," said Sita. "He was broken, smashed. There was a fight. I can't explain. My owner was against Lord Chiltern and his friends being in India. They killed a lot of us. Look out of the window. What do you see?" Hanuman looked. There below them in the gravel was a cannon.

"Can she sing?" said Charlie to Frank. "She looks great, she talks great. But can she sing? I love all that Indian dance thing and with the singing, it's so-o sexy."

"Hang on a bit there, Charlie, I'm just listening to what she's got to say."

"You mean you like her brains? We don't hire girls for their brains, do we?"

Sita and Hanuman looked at the cannon. "My owner was tied to the end of that cannon and then, in front of thousands of people, was shot to pieces."

Hanuman put his head in his hands. He couldn't believe it.

"And there is the man who gave the order to fire," said Sita turning and pointing to a picture of a man in uniform in the middle of one of the huge pictures. Underneath, it said: Lord Chiltern.

"But wasn't it a Lord Chiltern who was telling me about the shirts and the cotton?" said Hanuman.

"Yes," said Sita, "and because he was getting richer and richer while we were starving and dying, my owner was fighting."

Hanuman was still thinking about the dying and the fighting. "Oh dear," said Hanuman, "I never knew."

The moment Sita had used the word "fighting", there came a great cheer. It came from the glass case next to the picture of the men in uniform. In the glass case were nearly a hundred toy soldiers, in bright red uniforms. Charlie put his face up to the glass case and shouted at the little toy soldiers, "Stand by, guys, you're looking terrific. No one watching this movie is going to know you're not the real thing. Did you see 'Zulu'? No, don't worry about it. Make sure you lose things like wristwatches, ballpoint pens and the like. They didn't have stuff like that in those days, OK?"

This seemed to make the soldiers even more excited and they now started singing:

"On the 14th day of September
I remember well the date,
We showed the Pandies a new hit,
When we stormed the Kashmir Gate.
Their grapeshot, shell and musketry
They found but little good,
When British soldiers were outside
A-thirsting for their blood.
When a-hunting did we go, my boys,
A-hunting we did go.
To chase the Pandies night and day
And levelled Delhi low."

Then they all clapped and cheered again.

"What are they all singing about?" said Frank.

"Can't you guess?" said Sita. "The Pandies is what they called us. They love singing that stuff about 'thirsting for our blood.'"

Frank looked at what it said about them in the glass case: "The 52nd Infantry: their most glorious moment must surely have been the storming of the Kashmir Gate in the City of Delhi."

"Oh that!" said Sita, seeing Frank's blank look. "You don't know what it's about? It just means they killed lots of us."

Suddenly there was a huge roar of "CHARGE!" Alarm bells started ringing and they all heard a great clatter and a rush on the stairs outside.

"Stop thief!" came a shout and immediately afterwards the doors flew open.

Chapter  10

Dead Again

There stood Mr Butcher-in-armour with the sleek Dog.

"Don't move," roared this Mr Butcher, "we've seen it all on the closed circuit TV."

"You have?" said Charlie. "You have?" He was deliriously happy. He turned to Frank. "I knew you were the man for me, Frank. This is going to be a great partnership, me and you, as great a partnership as . . ." he waved his hands in the air . . . "as . . . as fish and chips."

The Dog looked up at Mr Butcher. "They have taken the priceless antique ivory statuette of Hanuman, the monkey-god."

"He wanted to find Sita," said Not-Sheba.

"Another of our priceless statuettes," snapped

the Dog.

"Why aren't you on your picture, girl?" said Mr Butcher-in-armour to Not-Sheba.

"Because she's going to co-star in a major new feature film, that's why, buddy-boy!" said Charlie looking round at Frank.

Frank was also looking round. He was looking round for a way out.

"If we lose the Pharaoh," said the Dog to Mr Butcher-in-armour, "a connection with the Chiltern family going back some two hundred years will be broken for ever. It would be a . . . tragedy." There was that trembly voice again.

"I am not a Pharaoh," said Charlie. "Will you stop telling people I'm a Pharaoh?"

Frank glanced out of the window. It was still open from when Sita had made them look out at the cannon.

"I don't know if you are aware, any of you," said Mr Butcher-in-armour, "but we have a strongroom here: a prison, in other words. We punish thieves and miscreants ourselves, right here. You, Frank, are unlikely ever to see your mother again."

Mr Butcher heaved his suit of armour closer, the Dog pulled back its lips and revealed a huge set of teeth.

Charlie looked at Frank. "If it's a pop video, we could have a singing dog, what do you think?"

"Please don't put me back on the picture, I can't stand another day of it there," said Not-Sheba.

"You should have thought of that before," said Mr Butcher-in-armour. "I've found over the years that Frank distracts not only himself but distracts everyone around him."

Oh, so it IS the real Mr Butcher! Or isn't it? Frank noticed that this Mr Butcher had the same tomato chin.

"But Frank's helping me find my name," said Not-Sheba.

Frank was backing slowly towards the window. Charlie was composing a boy-band, poppy sort of number . . . "Sha-wa-wa we can go on and on baby . . . sha-wa-wa . . ."

"Right," said the Dog, "seize the thieves." Mr Butcher and the Dog moved forwards.

Frank screamed at the top of his voice. "The window!" And grabbing Charlie with one arm and Not-Sheba with the other, he led them in a great daredevil leap straight out of the window.

"Take us, too," shouted Hanuman with a cry of bitter desperation . . . but it was too late. Frank, Not-Sheba and Charlie landed on the gravel next to the cannon and straight away started running.

"Frank, oh Frank baby, this is so last year," said Charlie. "A chase scene, for goodness sake! Every kind of chase has been done, don't you know that already? Helicopter chases man, cop-car chases thieves' car, lorry chases lorry, soldier chases prisoner, it's all been done. Yawn yawn yawn. This is your worst idea so far."

"Shut up and keep running," said Not-Sheba, "or you'll end up in a museum."

"Don't lose my worksheet, will you?" said Frank.

"Up here," said a voice.

They kept on running but looked up. "Up here, up the drainpipe and on to the roof." It was the Dolphin speaking. A large, metal dolphin leaned out of the gutter, its mouth wide open to let the rain water vomit out and into the drain-pipe. It had a very strong Yorkshire accent.

Not-Sheba climbed the drainpipe first, pulling herself up: hand, foot, hand, foot. Charlie went next, shouting, "People will say of me: 'And he did all his own stunts.'"

Frank came last. *Why do things keep getting so complicated?* All he wanted to do was just get on with the worksheet, but things kept interfering.

Not-Sheba had reached the top and climbed into the gutter, next to the Yorkshire Dolphin. Frank looked down. Frank wished he hadn't looked down. Then, just as he was thinking that he wished he hadn't looked down, he saw Mr Butcher-in-armour and the Dog come plodding along the gravel below.

"Quick," said Frank to Charlie just above him on the drainpipe, "they're coming."

Charlie was concentrating on making his climb look as spectacular as he could. "Perhaps I could be a stuntman as well," he said. "The legendary Charlie Chappin faced ordeal by fire, high-speed crashes and death by drowning.

He seemed immortal. Great stars paid tribute to him: Charlton Heston, Henry VIII, Goldilocks . . ."

"Charlie, look what you're doing," yelled Frank, "and don't lean back like that." Charlie was acting out receiving his Oscar while climbing up a drainpipe ten metres off the ground.

"Don't worry about me," said Frank grittily, "I was the Teletubbies' stuntman, you know."

"Charlie, look out!" shouted Not-Sheba from above, but it was too late. Charlie was losing his grip. Frank reached out for him and held him for a second, but he wasn't strong enough to hang on and Charlie lost his grip entirely, fell backwards off the drainpipe, his bandages flying in the air, and landed flat on his back on the gravel.

"Keep climbing, lads," called out the Dolphin.

"No, I've got to go back for him," said Frank, "I'm going to make him a star."

But a few seconds later Mr Butcher in his suit of armour and the Dog were on to Charlie. Frank, Not-Sheba and the Dolphin watched helplessly from ten metres up as Mr Butcher-in-armour and the dog stood over Charlie.

"He's dead," said Frank.

"He's been dead three thousand years," said Not-Sheba.

"But he's dead again," said Frank, realising the moment he said it that he had just talked nonsense. *But that doesn't matter here, does it?* He hauled himself up the last bit of the drainpipe and joined Not-Sheba and the Dolphin. They watched as Mr Butcher-in-armour and the Dog picked up the limp figure of Charlie. "Oh this is awful," said Frank. "It was my fault. I had him by the hand but I just couldn't hold on."

Mr Butcher-in-armour and the Dog looked up. "We'll be back, don't you worry," said Mr Butcher. "You won't get away with this."

Do Not Boil

"You've been useless," said Not-Sheba to Frank. He looked across at her. *Why is it that the moment I feel bad about one thing, there is always someone nearby who can make me feel even worse?* "You haven't got anywhere near finding my name," she said.

"What do you want a name for?" said the Dolphin. "I haven't got a name. Never bothered me." Frank noticed that the Dolphin's metal skin was mottled with bits of lichen growing on it.

"Yes, but that's not the only thing he's useless at," said Not-Sheba.

I hate her.

"We were going to make a film," she said, "but now the major star has been taken off to have his stomach looked at by scientists."

"What? What?" said Frank. "How do you know that that's what they're doing?" he said.

"Oh, that's what they always do with mummies, isn't it?" said Not-Sheba. "They keep opening them up to find out what the last thing they ate was. And it's always bits of wheat. Everyone must have always been eating wheat. I've never understood what's so tasty about it myself."

She must have picked up an enormous amount of knowledge sitting up there on that painting listening to people, Frank thought.

"I prefer drawing," said the Dolphin.

"What? More than eating wheat?" said Not-Sheba. "That's good. You're quite a sensible dolphin, then."

"If you prefer drawing," said Frank, quick to grab an opportunity, "you can help me with the worksheet. There's quite a few things I've got to draw on that."

"How are you going to help *me*?" said the Dolphin.

Frank wasn't very knowledgeable about

helping dolphins but he tried to come up with a few suggestions all the same. "I can clean cars, do the washing up or weed your garden. Me and my friend Tony do jobs for people to get pocket money."

"No," said the Dolphin, "I don't have much need for that. What I'd really like is for someone to sit up here and read to me. I really like being read to. You see, I sit up here and I hear people down below reading out their Chiltern House leaflets and guidebooks to each other. It was all right once or twice, but I've heard it about twenty-five thousand times and it's driving me crazy now. If I hear: 'Stand facing the West Front, look up and you will see the dolphin. It was made by hand out of lead from the Chiltern lead mines in Ribley,' once more, I will go crazy. I will blow up."

Frank looked at the Dolphin and wondered what this Dolphin would look like, blown up.

"Do you mean blown apart or blown up?" he said. "If you were blown up you'd look like a huge balloon . . . like an airship."

The Dolphin didn't seem to hear and went on grumbling, "It's not even as if Lord Chiltern made me. Arnold made me."

"Maybe your name's Arnold," said Frank to Not-Sheba.

"Arnold made me," the Dolphin went on, "but it was hundreds of lads and lasses and their kiddies who got the lead out: Albert, Edith, Sissie, Rachel, Grace, Reuben, Davy, Lizzie, Meg, Sarah—"

"Any of those?" said Frank to Not-Sheba. "Maybe you used to make lead."

"— Florrie, Billy, Charles, Georgie, Mo, Amy, Little Arnold, Ben, Mary, Wilbur . . ." The Dolphin chuntered on and on. Frank and Not-Sheba gazed at it, amazed.

"Maybe you should read to us, instead of us reading to you," said Not-Sheba.

That stopped the Dolphin. "Yes, that's right — read to me," said the Dolphin. "That's what you were going to do."

"I haven't got anything to read to you," said Frank, "except the labels on my clothes."

"That'll do," said the Dolphin.

Frank began. "Size S, made in Portugal, do not boil."

"Do not boil?" said the Dolphin. "Do not boil? It sounds like a cooking recipe. What do they expect? That you're going to eat your knickers?"

"Do not bleach, do not spin, do not wring. Pull into shape while damp. Dry flat. Warm iron. Do not iron rubber motif."

"Right lovely," said the Dolphin.

"These jeans are designed to fade and lose colour. Therefore take the following precautions: always wash separately, don't use bleach, pull legs to original length after washing."

"Very wise," said the Dolphin.

"I haven't got much else," said Frank.

"How about you?" said the Dolphin to Not-Sheba.

"No, nothing."

"That's lies," said Frank, "she's got my worksheet."

"Oh, I love worksheets," said the Dolphin. "Stuff like: 'Read the questions carefully, and don't use felt tips', lovely stuff. Come on then, love."

Not-Sheba wouldn't take the worksheet out. "She's afraid I'll grab it off her," said Frank, "and then run away. I'm supposed to be helping her with her name."

"Well, you sit this side o' me . . . and you can sit t'other side," said the Dolphin to them, "and now begin."

Not-Sheba had folded the worksheet up so she started at page three. "Stand facing the West Front, look up and you will see a Dolphin. It was made by Lord Chiltern. What is it made of? Where did he get his material from?"

The Dolphin started yelling. "What did I say? What did I say? Why are you doing this to me? First of all I tell you I can't stand hearing that rubbish. Then I tell you it's blithering well wrong anyway. I shall go mad. I can't stand it. What's the matter? Don't you believe me? Do you think I'm a liar? Is that it? Right, you two, get on my back. Go on, get on my back."

"No, look—" said Frank, "I've got to get on with my worksheet, and get back to the coach—"

"Do as I tell you," shouted the Dolphin, "and you."

"No, all I'm doing is trying to find out my name," said Not-Sheba.

"Get on now," said the Dolphin, "or I'll fling you off this roof. Hold on tight, and let's go-o-o-o-o-o."

The Dolphin took off like a great clumsy, heavy bird with Frank and Not-Sheba hanging on for dear life.

Chapter 12

Dogs, Eagles, Suns

The Dolphin swooped up over Chiltern House and they could see the gardens, temples and monuments below them. The Dolphin had calmed down by now.

Frank leaned over to Not-Sheba and whispered, "I'm really not worried that this Dolphin can fly."

"You look like you are," said Not-Sheba.

"I always fancied me hand at aerial photography, you know."

"Could you try not to swerve about quite so much?" said Frank. "It makes me get a sick feeling in my stomach."

"And then I could sell the photos. I'd offer to take aerial pictures of people's houses and backyards. I could make quite a good living out of that, you know."

On they flew. The landscape changed and now they were flying over rivers and roads.

"I'll avoid the towns," said the Dolphin. "Some chump is bound to report us to the police." Cars crawled along roads, and rivers wrinkled over rocks. They flew over woods and valleys, villages and hills.

"Lord Chiltern used to own all this, hundreds of years ago," said the Dolphin.

"You're swerving again," said Frank.

"We're heading for t'moors, now."

"Well it's better than being stuck in a picture with Master William and Miss Charlotte," said Not-Sheba.

And still they flew on, the wind rushing in their ears. Not-Sheba pulled herself closer to Frank. He was glad she did.

"Ribley!" shouted the Dolphin. "This is where I came from." They looked down and beneath them was a hard, rugged mountain, too high for trees to grow on. It looked scarred and pock-marked. The Dolphin nodded at the holes in the hillside. "That's the lead mines where Albert, Reuben, Davy, Billy, Charles —"

"Oh no, spare us," said Not-Sheba, "not that lot again."

"And look, see that. See those ruins? Do you know what they are?"

"Ruins," said Frank, his mind working like a worksheet.

"Those are all that's left of the barracks where the miners lived during the week. Pretty rough, they were. Freezin' in winter, bakin' hot in summer. Nowt on t'floor."

"Didn't it have a roof on?" said Not-Sheba.

"Ruins," said the Dolphin. "That's all that's left of where they had to sleep. They went home at weekends. Oh, I'd love to draw that."

"When we get back, you can draw it on my worksheet," said Frank.

"I know," said the Dolphin, "and no felt tips."

"Can we go back now?" said Not-Sheba.

"Hang on, I haven't shown you where the kids worked."

"No swerving," said Frank "or I'll be sick."

"There," said the Dolphin. "Little kids used to

sort the rocks there."

"Nice," said Frank.

"Nice?" said the Dolphin. "I'd like to see you try it. Working till your fingers bled and you were fit to drop."

"I wouldn't wait till my fingers bled. I'd just do the 'drop' bit."

"No, you wouldn't. Your mum would be pushing you to keep going, because she needed the money."

"Oh, I'd go round to my Nan's."

"She'd be working alongside you."

"I give up," said Frank.

"You can't," said the Dolphin, "this is the only way you can get money to live."

"No, I mean, I give up now. Let's go back to Chiltern House."

The Dolphin was getting carried away. "Chiltern House? These are all Chiltern's Houses, if you like. That's why you lived here. If you didn't work in the Chiltern Mines, you got chucked out of your Chiltern House. The little tiny house you lived in was a Chiltern house too, you know."

"No," said Frank, " I mean the Chiltern House we were in before. Where you sit on the roof all day with your mouth open."

"That's right," said the Dolphin, "and there are thousands of us, sitting with our mouths open on the roofs of big houses all over the country. All of 'em good Chiltern lead."

"Time to go back now," said Not-Sheba.

"Right you are," said the Dolphin. "Now you've seen it: Ribley and the Great Chiltern lead mines."

"I don't think I came from there," said Not-Sheba.

"I'd love to take a great big wide-angle aerial photo of that lot," said the Dolphin, heading back to the big Chiltern House. "I'd put it up in the Great Hall so everyone could see what made Chiltern House."

"I thought . . ." said Frank, but his voice petered out. He was thinking about what happened in the chapel. "I thought . . ." and again his voice petered out but this time he was thinking about what that Mr Butcher person said to Hanuman before he let him pass. *It's very*

111

confusing, this business of 'what made Chiltern House'.

Back they flew towards it, with Frank's mind now wandering over the thousands of lead dolphins sitting on the tops of buildings all over the country. *They'd be worth a lot*, he thought. "Were they all dolphins?" said Frank as they flew over forests and villages.

"No. Drains, gutters, church roofs, dogs, eagles, suns, all sorts."

As they got near to the great house, an unpleasant sight greeted them. There on the roof where the Dolphin was going to land, stood the Mr Butcher in the suit of armour, the Dog and about a hundred toy soldiers.

"Don't land there!" shouted Not-Sheba.

"I have to," said the Dolphin.

"No, you don't," said Not-Sheba. "Sure you don't."

"I'm tied to the house. There's nothing I can do about it. I'm Chiltern lead for Chiltern House."

"Slave!" shouted Not-Sheba, as the Dolphin swooped down towards its place on the roof.

"We've got them now," roared Mr Butcher,

"FIRE!" And the little toy soldiers fired off their little muskets and rifles.

Frank and Not-Sheba were peppered all over with tiny little bullets, each one no more than a pinprick, but with so many, it was really painful.

The Dolphin swooped nearer and nearer. "They've got chains!" shouted Not-Sheba. "They're going to chain us up."

The toy soldiers were singing:

"Their grapeshot, shell and musketry
They found but little good,
When British soldiers were outside
A-thirsting for their blood."

"Sorry," said the Dolphin, and landed in its place on the roof. Mr Butcher and the Dog seized Not-Sheba and Frank.

"I'll never finish my worksheet now," said Frank.

Not-Sheba wasn't cowed. She started yelling at this Mr Butcher-in-armour: "Oh, go lock yourself in your helmet, Rustybum. And the next time you want to speak you'll have to use a tin-opener to get your head out."

Mr Butcher-in-armour shook his fist. The Dog

snarled and said, "Your friend will be taken to a museum, cut open and examined in great detail in order to find out what he ate three thousand years ago."

"You were right," said Frank.

"He was eating your peanut butter sandwich when we were in India, wasn't he, Frank?" said Not-Sheba.

"Was he?" said Frank.

Chapter 13

Stifling the Scream

"To the strongroom," said Mr Butcher-in-armour, "quick march!"

"What do you think they'll get for this?" said the Dog. "Transportation? A few years of hard labour in Australia would do them the world of good."

"Sounds good enough to me," said Mr Butcher-in-armour. "Thieving has to be dealt with very seriously."

Frank and Not-Sheba were marched across the roof and down several flights of stairs. "I was getting on with the worksheet," said Frank, "really I was, sir."

"Too late now, boy," Mr Butcher-in-armour

said, and pulled his helmet shut.

"I knew this would happen," said Not-Sheba.

"What've you done with Charlie?" said Frank, "I mean, the mummy?"

"It's been packaged up for the university museum," said the Dog.

"And we're going to Australia, are we?"

"We'll see what the judge says," said the Dog. "You'll get a fair trial."

By now, they were down in the basement. Mr Butcher opened a door. Not-Sheba and Frank were pushed inside and the door slammed and locked behind them. The only light was the thin line that came in under the door. Everything was getting too much for Frank. All he wanted was to be back on the coach, going home and, if necessary, being dropped on the scrap heap. Anything rather than this. He felt tired, alone and scared.

"I'm tired and lonely," said Frank.

"Me too," said Not-Sheba.

"Are you scared?" said Frank

"No," said Not-Sheba.

"I am," said Frank.

Not-Sheba put her arm round him and he leant towards her. It felt nice but he felt like crying. "I'm sure we'll be all right," said Not-Sheba.

"I'm not so sure," said Frank.

Everything was so dark. Then came the noise. It was a kind of syrupy, dripping noise. A kind of bubble-in-mud noise.

"I know what this is," said Frank. "They're going to drown us. They're going to fill the place up with water. And we won't be able to get out. We're just going to drown in here."

The ghastly syrupy noise went on, but now there were more bubbles. It sounded like something was coming alive in mud. Suddenly, Frank felt a cold, damp hand close round his neck. He screamed. The hand moved to his mouth, stifling the scream. There was a horrible, gurgling sound in his ear and Frank heard a voice say, "This is the first day of your death."

Not-Sheba was breathing fast in the dark. They could see nothing.

Then the voice said, "I'll get an Oscar for this,

117

Frank, you know. 'The Mummy Strikes Back.' Best motion picture, best leading actor, best cold damp hands."

"Charlie, it's you!" shouted Not-Sheba in a voice that showed how glad she was. "So they haven't packaged you up yet!"

Frank was still shaking.

"I'll turn the light on," said Charlie.

"You mean it could have been light in here all this time?" said Frank.

"Sure," said Charlie, "but I like the dark effect. Don't you remember 'Alien II?'"

Charlie switched on the light. There was a moment of relief. Not-Sheba and Frank relaxed back and then suddenly Frank sat bolt upright and screamed. There, about an arm's length away from Frank's face, was a large glass jar, the size of a bucket. In the jar was a man's head. It blinked, and a few bubbles came out of its mouth. *That's what made the horrible noise*, thought Frank.

"Don't point, Frank," said Not-Sheba, "it's rude." She was staring very hard at the head. "Frank, don't you see? Look, look, look. He's black. I think I'm going to get the answer. I just feel it."

"Do Oscar winners get a lot of money Frank?" said Charlie, and then, not waiting for an answer: "I'll spend it on fizzy water. Gallons and gallons of fizzy water. I love fizzy water. I love the way it bubbles on your tongue and then a few minutes later, makes you burp."

Not-Sheba moved closer to the head. "Who are you?" she said to it.

"Pemulwuy," bubbled the head.

"Where do you come from?"

"Australia," he said.

"Australia?" said Frank. "They told us we might go to Australia. Is it nice there?"

The head moved slowly. "It might be nice now. I don't know," he said. "When people were transported there it was hell for them. If you're transported, you'll be chained together and work all day in the boiling sun, stone-breaking till you drop dead with exhaustion."

"Were you transported?" said Frank.

The head smiled sadly. "My friend, my people reached Australia forty thousand years ago."

"That's older than you, Charlie," said Frank.

"I'm a rising young star," said Charlie.

"How come you're here now?" said Not-Sheba to the head in the jar.

"I was a rebel. Lord Chiltern's younger son came out to Australia to seek his fortune. Whenever he tried to clear the forests, he found that there were people living there already: my people, the Koorie. So he killed us. We fought back. Sometimes we won. We raided their places at night, and took away the animals they put in our country. They shot at us. I was shot through seven times. They chained me up but I escaped with the chains still round my legs. My people came to believe that nothing could kill me. Again and again we raided their places.

"It wasn't only us they were terrible to. I saw them doing things to their own people. Time and again we watched from the bush and saw them beating naked men with long whips till their backs were just streaming with blood. First they brought them to our country in chains, and if they did anything wrong – like talk when they were eating – they beat them till

120

they were nearly dead. If they were doing such murderous things to each other, I suppose it was small wonder they did the same or worse to us.

"When they got me, they killed me, beheaded me and sent my head back to the young man's father. I was a present. A novelty for visitors to this Great House to admire."

Not-Sheba listened, fascinated. "Am I a Koorie?" she asked.

Pemulwuy stared at her. "No," he said. "Once they sent soldiers after us and amongst them was a man who wasn't like the white men. He was black like you."

"Where did he come from?" said Not-Sheba in a hurry.

"As far as I know," said Pemulwuy, "England."

"Oh no," said Not-Sheba, "I thought I was so near and now I'm so far."

"Yes," said Charlie, "'A Bridge Too Far'. Great war film. Frank! Frank!"

Frank was still thinking about what Pemulwuy had said.

"Frank — a war movie. Why didn't we think of

it?" Charlie went into a film dialogue:

"The tanks are moving westwards, Robson."

"Have they got air-cover, sir?"

"HQ on the line. HQ on the line."

"Tea with two sugars, sir. No biscuits left, sir. We used them to mend the holes in the tank sir."

"Shut up, Charlie," said Not-Sheba, still concentrating on Pemulwuy.

Frank was looking round the strongroom. It was a junk room now, piled high with all the odds and ends and old collections that the Chilterns hadn't put on show upstairs. Bicycles, books, model boats, paintings, vases, old shoes. Heaps of it. Frank got up and began to look at what there was.

Charlie turned to Not-Sheba. "You know they want to dissect my stomach? Wykham Scientific Film Unit are planning to make a documentary film. I can see it now. The scalpel cut across my stomach, the slow peel back of the skin, the incision into the stomach, the careful removal of the material. The deadly serious commentary: '. . . the contents of the ancient Egyptian priest's stomach were removed and an extensive series of tests were run . . .'"

"Hey, what are these?" said Frank, as he opened an old cupboard. Inside, dozens of little straw figures were dancing up and down.

"I will have the world's most famous belly-button," said Charlie.

Chapter 14

A Knife through his Hand

Not-Sheba wanted to go on talking to Pemul-wuy. Charlie was making documentary science films and Frank was watching the dancing straw figures. Some of them looked like little women.

"What are you doing here?" said Frank.

"Lady Chiltern collected us," said one, "but they got bored with us and put us in a cup-board."

"But what are you?" said Frank.

"Corn dollies," said another of them.

Charlie was doing a running commentary to a nature film: "Here on the forest floor, we see the giant stag beetle meet its old enemy the rhinoceros beetle. In a matter of seconds, they become locked in combat . . ."

"What's a corn dolly?" said Frank.

"Us," said a corn dolly.

"What do corn dollies do?" said Frank.

"We are the queens of the harvest. My name's Harvest Queen, you know."

"My name's Mother Earth," said another.

"I'm Ivy Girl."

"I'm Harvest Dame."

"I'm Frank," said Frank.

"Oh, we all know about you," said the corn dollies, "you've been thieving."

"I wasn't. That's lies."

"That's what they all say," said Harvest Dame. "We've had all sorts in here, you know."

Meanwhile, Pemulwuy was telling Not-Sheba a story. ". . . when they came to look for us, we could just disappear into the bush. We knew every tree, every track. Once a party of troopers came into the bush. We would listen and they wouldn't know we were there. They were afraid of every insect, every leaf. They were afraid they'd die of thirst. But we knew which insects to eat. We knew which plants to cut open and suck. It was our place. So they went back to their camps. They knew they couldn't hunt us by tracking us. Next day, they burnt the forests and when we ran out and away from the flames, they shot at us: men, women and children . . . all of us . . ."

"Did you escape that time?" said Not-Sheba.

Charlie joined Frank with the corn dollies.

"Who else has been in here?" said Frank.

"Little Arnold," said Mother Earth.

"Little Arnold? Little Arnold? I've heard of him."

"Me too," said Charlie, "Little Arnold Schwarzenegger, Mr Universe. Terminator. Strong man. I was thinking of getting him to appear in one of my movies. I was going to dress him up in a bear suit and do 'King Kong versus the Giant Grizzly', but then I heard he went into politics. I was going to play King Kong. Have they done a remake of 'King Kong'?"

"No, yes, no," said Mother Earth, "Little Arnold was one of the lead miners."

"That's it," said Frank, "I knew I'd heard of

him from somewhere. Why was he here?"

"He stole some lead ore: rock with lead in it."

"Why did he do that?"

"Because he wasn't getting enough money mining, so he thought he'd make a bit of money on the side. He did want to eat, after all."

"What happened to him?" said Frank, "Did they send him to Australia too?"

"No," said the corn dolly called Harvest Dame.

"Well?" said Frank, "What happened to him?" There was silence. Nobody wanted to say. "Come on," said Frank, "tell me, I have to know. It might happen to us."

"Oh no," said Harvest Dame, "it only happened to lead miners."

"Well, tell me all the same."

Charlie stepped nearer. He was trying to make himself look like a detective.

"Do you know what a supergrass is, young lady?"

"No," said Harvest Dame.

"You play ball with us, we play ball with you. Know what I mean? You plead guilty, we tell the judge that you've helped us put the five villains in the slammer, you go down for five years instead of ten years. Know what I mean? And we'll forget about the Barclays Bank job, right? Eh? Know what I mean?"

"What's he talking about?" said Harvest Dame.

"I'm making a film with him," said Frank, almost believing himself.

"You're in it as well," said Charlie to the corn dollies. "What can they be?"

Frank looked at them. He was still wondering about what happened to Little Arnold.

". . . they built fences. We didn't know what fences were," said Pemulwuy from his jar, "we didn't know you could say: "This piece of land is mine," and put a fence round it. The land is like the air and the sea. It belongs to everyone. You can't put a fence round it and say it belongs to you. They kept trying to tell us we should have the bit over there, or the bit over the other side of the mountain. But everywhere was everybody's. They didn't understand that, so they shot us . . ."

"Can you do Kung Fu?" said Charlie to the corn dollies. "You could be the Kung Fu gang in a Bruce Lee movie. He's dead, but his spirit lives on. I'm going to be the next Bruce Lee." Charlie went through a few King Fu moves, yelled "Ah Chah" and brought his hand down hard on to Frank's right leg.

"Great," said Frank, "I won't be able to walk for a week."

"That's nothing to what'll happen to you later," said Mother Earth.

"Look here," said Frank, "How come you know so much? Who are you, anyway?"

"Oh don't mind us," said Harvest Dame. "The farm workers made us at harvest time. Lord Chiltern's farms spread from here to the lead mines, so that's one huge lot of corn dollies. There's only forty-three of us here now. There must have been hundreds of us every year once upon a time. When Lord Chiltern's man came round to collect the rent off the farm people, Lady Chiltern used to collect us."

"Ah chah!" said Charlie and kicked the wall.

"Sh-sh-sh," said the corn dollies, "they'll come down here if you make a noise. Remember what happened to Little Arnold."

"Yes," said Frank. "I mean, no. You never did say what happened to Little Arnold."

"You tell him," said Harvest Dame to Ivy Girl.

"No," said Ivy Girl. "You tell him," she said to the one called Maiden.

"I'll tell him," said Little Moppet. "They tied him to the winding gear at the top of the mine. You know, the thing like the handle you wind a bucket up out of a well with. Well, they stuck a knife through his hand, into the wooden bit of the winding gear and left him."

"But he could pull the knife out, couldn't he?" said Frank.

"No, he was tied up wasn't he?"

". . . they came and chopped the land up into little bits but no matter what we did, whether we talked with them or whether we fought them, there was never any land for us. They just kept telling us, we could go over there, or over the other way . . ."

Not-Sheba's eyes stared at Pemulwuy's head in the jar, as he said these things.

Frank was looking at his hand, imagining it with a knife stuck through it, into a piece of wood. "I'll just keep saying I wasn't taking Hanuman away. I was only taking him back to India."

"I'm just the sheriff," said Charlie. "Tell your story to the judge, Monday morning."

There was a rattle of keys, the lock turned and the door opened. In the light stood the Dog and the platoon of toy soldiers.

"Prisoner Frank, prisoner Sheba, prisoner mummified Pharaoh, you are summoned to court. Quick march — left, right, left, right, left . . ." And Charlie, Frank and Not-Sheba were marched out of the room and down a corridor.

"Have you still got my worksheet?" said Frank to Not-Sheba.

"Martians are not invincible, Captain," said Charlie, "Earth to Venus. We have high frequency interference on the Z band. Over and out . . . The corn dollies can be the Martians," said Charlie

131

excitedly.

"Yes, Charlie," said Frank. "Yes," he said, hoping that just for once, just for one blessed once that Charlie would shut up. He just wanted to have time to think about all the horrible things that were about to happen to him.

Not-Sheba was deep in thought. "I still don't know who I am," she said.

"We could cover my mummy case in silver paper, hold it up in the air at night and it would look like a space ship," said Charlie. "Special Effects, Frank, Special Effects."

"Special Effects," said Frank in a dream, "Special Effects."

A Little Black Lady

On down the corridor they marched, the Dog behind, the soldiers in front, their little feet tip-tapping on the stone floors. All along the walls, swords and guns were mounted on display.

"We land on a planet," said Charlie, "lost in time. We have arrived in a different era, but we have modern technology. 'God's wounds,' says an old man, looking at my laser ray gun. 'I would fain wield such a machine i' faith.' 'Yay,' I say, 'but I have a laser gun and an H-bomb and you have a club and boots. Hard cheese, buddy.' And I dematerialise him."

"I'm sorry I didn't help you find your name," said Frank to Not-Sheba.

"That's OK," she said. "I didn't get on very well with your worksheet."

"Yep," said Frank, "I'm for the scrap heap."

"The scrap heap's probably paradise compared with where we're going."

"Hmmm," said Frank, looking down at the toy soldiers marching on ahead. They were singing their Indian song:

"Their grapeshot, shell and musketry,

they found but little good,

when British soldiers were outside

A-thirsting for their blood."

"You're only toy soldiers, you know," shouted Frank. "You're not real – you're made of – er – what are they made of?" said Frank.

"I don't know," said Not-Sheba.

"I'll de-materialise them," said Charlie.

"What are you made of?" shouted Frank to the soldiers.

One of them called back to him over the singing: "Lead."

"What does that make you think of?" said Frank to Not-Sheba, expecting her to say the Dolphin.

"Little Moppet," said Not-Sheba.

"Little Moppet, what's she got to do with it?"

"What she said about Little Arnold and that thing about his hand . . ."

And Charlie added helpfully, "You remember: Little Arnold Schwarzenegger."

"Yes," said Frank to both of them.

By now they had reached two large double doors. "Wait here until you are called," said the Dog and it pushed past them and through the doors.

"We face the intergalactic overlord with calm determination," said Charlie, and he added anxiously, "you don't think all this intergalactic stuff was done to death with 'Toy Story', do you? I really worry sometimes that I sound so last-year."

Then, just a moment later, the doors were flung open and the Dog led the three prisoners into a large courtroom. The judge's chair was empty but in front of it, on a table, stood Hanuman and Sita. In front of that, at a desk sat Mrs Morrell, Frank's teacher. On benches, sat Miss Charlotte and Master William, Father

Abbot, the Dolphin and many more toy soldiers.

Miss Charlotte and Master William waved at Not-Sheba. She looked at them, at first with surprise and then turned her head away. Frank looked at her and could see that it upset her to see them looking so jolly and carefree while she was in such trouble, and in public too.

"Stand for his Lordship, Justice Chiltern!" said the Dog, and Mr Butcher-in-armour clanked in, with his helmet on and a judge's wig stuck on the top. He eased himself down into the chair and looked around him.

The Dog spoke up: "The case before us today, m'lud, concerns the attempted theft of the priceless Indian statuette that you see before you. The accused are Sheba from the painting, the mummified Pharaoh from the North corridor, and Frank."

"How do you plead?" said Mr Butcher

"Not guilty," said Not-Sheba.

"Not guilty," said Frank.

Charlie remained silent.

"How do you plead?" said Mr Butcher. Still Charlie remained silent. "I shall assume you plead guilty if you remain silent. For the last time: How do you plead?"

"I am not a mummified Pharaoh," said Charlie.

"What are you then?" said Mr Butcher.

Frank held his breath. Which one of his many characters would Charlie choose? The mummified priest? Charlie Chappin? The detective? There was a pause.

"What are you?" said Mr Butcher.

"Queen Victoria," said Charlie.

Frank blinked.

"And how do you plead?" said Mr Butcher

"Not guilty," said Charlie.

"Proceed," said Mr Butcher and the Dog began.

"The accused were apprehended by means of the closed circuit TV system."

Charlie interrupted, forgetting to sound like Queen Victoria. "Release the video! Get it into the stores! Let people hire it – now!"

The Dog ignored Charlie. "On looking at the CCTV evidence, we became aware that Hanuman was being removed from his proper place by the three accused. When we entered the Indian Room, they were holding Hanuman – to be precise, Frank was. Standing before you, m'lud, are three wicked villains, who don't care one jot for the staggering beauty or the extraordinary value of this priceless statuette, villains who were prepared to wreck the wonderful Chiltern House collection for their own greedy ends. And, the Chiltern House collection, let it be said, is not some small amateur assortment of curios. No. It is a glorious display of a great family's history, recording its worldwide exploits, achievements and successes; its glorious array of beautiful works of art. All in all, Chiltern House and its collection is almost a history of Britain itself. And these villains were intent upon wrecking it. It is too horrible to contemplate. I call for the severest sentence." And the Dog sat down.

Master William and Miss Charlotte clapped frantically, followed by Mr Butcher-the-judge, who then stopped himself by shouting, "Order, order."

"He'll never get the part," whispered Charlie

in Frank's ear. "Throw him off the set, Frank."

Frank was staring at the judge. Now he looked more like his teacher. "What do you say for yourselves?" said Mr Butcher. "I am not going to send letters home to your parents until I've heard your side of the story."

Not-Sheba spoke up. "This is all rubbish. How could you say we stole Hanuman? You stole Hanuman from a Portuguese ship three hundred years ago."

Hanuman shouted, "And the Portuguese stole it from Goa thirty years before that."

"Order, order!" shouted Mr Butcher. "That's all history, and nothing to do with what we're talking about. Frank?"

"We were just taking him back to India, sir," said Frank.

"India?" said Mr Butcher, "India? You're supposed to be on the coach by 3.30. How were you going to get to India and back?"

"Ah, India," said Charlie in his Queen Victoria voice, "I am Empress of India."

"Are you trying to say, in your own muddled, stupid way, you were taking Hanuman up to the

Indian room?" said Mr Butcher. Frank was really struggling to work out which Butcher this was and it wasn't made any easier by the fact that his eyes seemed to be covered in some kind of film of water.

"Yes, sir," said Frank.

"What did we learn yesterday in assembly?"

Frank recited, "No shouting, no running, no touching–"

"Stop there," said Mr Butcher. "No touching. Whatever could have got into you to make you think that you could move the Chiltern House statues?"

"It wasn't my idea," said Frank. "It was his," he said, pointing to Hanuman, but the moment he said it, he felt terrible, telling on Hanuman like that.

"So in the letter to your mother, Frank, I shall write: 'Frank didn't steal the statue, it was the statue's idea.' Very believable, lad."

"But it's true," shouted Hanuman.

"Order, order!" shouted Mr Butcher. "And you, Sheba, I'm surprised. After all we've done for you. Brought you here, given you a fine and beautiful house to grow up in, taught you the accomplishments of an English lady and you treat us like this." And under his breath he whispered to the Dog: "It's the savage coming out in her, you know."

"I heard that," shouted Not-Sheba. "Lady Chiltern might have taught me how to sew. The tutor might have taught me how to read and write and play that damn harpsichord but no one has told me who I really am. You taught me all that so I could pretend to be somebody I wasn't. Not for my sake – for yours. So I could be a dainty little lady – but oh how sweet – black. A little black lady to put on show. A little black lady you made. But you can't make people like you can make a robot, like you can make Frankenstein's monster."

Wow, thought Frank, *she must have listened so hard to people's conversations over the years, up on that painting. What kind of person would have walked round Chiltern House talking about Frankenstein?*

The mention of Frankenstein had an immediate effect on Charlie. He started grunting and swinging his arms to and fro. He grabbed hold of the table in front of him and started to smash it up.

"If only I had a bolt through my head," he whispered to Frank.

"Order, order!" shouted Mr Butcher. "If you say anything else, Sheba, I shall cut your tongue out."

More claps and cheers from William and Charlotte. Not-Sheba sucked her teeth at them.

"Right," said Mr Butcher, "I've heard enough, you are all three guilty. I will think for three seconds what the sentences will be . . . Frank, you will be transported to Australia for ten years to serve hard labour for five of them."

"Sheeeesh," said Frank.

"Queen Victoria, we have reason to believe you are not Queen Victoria. As a mummified Pharaoh, you will be taken to Manchester University archaeology department for internal examination and a TV programme will be made about you called 'The Chiltern Mummy'."

"I demand the right to choose the director of the movie. I want it down on the contract. You don't think Tom Cruise would sign away his body like this, do you?"

"Silence!" shouted Mr Butcher.

"But you, Sheba, will not have these privileges. You will go back to where you came from, and never show your ungrateful face here again." Mr Butcher got ready to go.

Not-Sheba shouted, "But where do I come from? No one's ever told me."

Mr Butcher sat down again. He looked less like Frank's teacher at this moment. There was a long pause. Frank found himself holding his breath. He realised that he wanted to know the answer to Sheba's question too. This Mr Butcher began: "Originally you came from somewhere in Africa, Sheba. I can't say as I know exactly because I bought you from a trader in Guinea and he didn't tell me and I didn't ask. You were taken to my plantation in Jamaica, but I saved your life, you know. Half way across the Atlantic, when the seas were rough, we had to lighten our load and I ordered some twenty or thirty of your fellow slaves to be thrown overboard. I caught sight of you and ordered the Captain not to throw you too. When we landed in Jamaica,

I took you to my plantation and again, I helped you. Instead of working you in the fields like the other slaves, I had you brought indoors to work in the house and then when I returned to England, I brought you with me. And that is saying something, my girl. I gave you all this —". at this Mr Butcher waved his hand in the air, and out towards the windows and the Chiltern House grounds . . .

Not-Sheba listened spellbound. But instead of answering the questions it just made her ask more.

"But who was my mother? Where did I live? And what is my real name?"

Mr Butcher got up to go. "As I've said to you, these were not questions we asked the traders in the slave markets. I chose you for your bright eyes, good teeth and broad back. I thought you'd make a good worker, one day."

Not-Sheba couldn't believe it. So near and so far again.

Charlie came over to her, "You see, you could've come from Egypt after all. Egypt's in Africa. We might be relatives."

For the very first time in all this, Frank had a feeling that Charlie might be talking sense.

Not-Sheba waved him aside. She wasn't interested. Frank looked at her and could see that things were spinning round in her head.

"So where are you sending me?" said Not-Sheba to Mr Butcher as he was leaving.

"Oh, Jamaica, of course. We don't send slaves back to Africa," and he left.

The Dog stepped forward with the soldiers and they got ready to march Frank, Not-Sheba and Charlie off when, suddenly, there was a huge roar and a shout, and through the double doors and the windows came the corn dollies, the heads from the chapel and carried high, amongst them all, Pemulwuy.

Don't Shoot

"What is going on?" shouted the Mr Butcher-in-armour.

On rushed the corn dollies and the heads. Before he could say much more, Mr Butcher-in-armour was surrounded and seized. A moment later the Dog was too. Two corn dollies unwound some straw and tied up its mouth.

"You can't do this," said Mr Butcher-in-armour. "Soldiers, to your positions."

Little Moppet leapt up. "Soldiers, don't shoot. Look what you are made of. You come from the earth just as we do. When the people who made us starved, the people who made you starved too. Would you kill your own mothers and fathers, your own brothers and sisters? No, don't shoot!"

"Shoot!" yelled Mr Butcher-in-armour, "Kill them!"

Hanuman and Pemulwuy joined in. "Don't shoot, soldiers. You don't have to do what he says. You're like us. Join us."

"This didn't happen in 'Star Wars', did it?" said Charlie. "Or 'Winnie the Pooh'."

"No," said Frank trying to imagine Winnie the Pooh and Piglet running through the Hundred Acre Wood with a bunch of soldiers.

The soldiers muttered amongst themselves. Some made a move towards Mr Butcher.

Harvest Queen spoke up, "This court is abolished. It does not exist. It is finished." And there was a huge cheer.

"Lord Chiltern," said one of the heads with his big grinning face, "you are under arrest."

"I am?" said Mr Butcher. "What've I done wrong?"

Frank had a feeling that there was something wrong with the question itself. *It's OK that he wants to know about stuff being 'wrong' but it's not just him, is it?*

Not him, on his own. It's all the Butchers . . . or Chilterns . . . whichever they are . . . I can't even work out which one is which any more. Armour, admiral, judge, or what?

"As far as we're concerned, it's this:" said one of the heads. "For hundreds of years you put fences round the land where we grazed our sheep and cows, round the woods we put our pigs in. You put fences round the land that we all used and then you said it was yours. We've pulled down the fences. The land on that hill you see out of the window belongs to all of us again."

Everyone cheered, especially Pemulwuy bubbling away in his jar.

"That's our story," said Ivy Girl to Mr Butcher. "Maybe some of the others have got things to say — Pemulwuy? Hanuman? Dolphin? Not-Sheba?"

Before they had time to answer, Charlie started shouting, "This is news, man, and we're here. Grab it, grab it. When it hits the world's TV screens tonight it'll be a sensation. Ring the producer, tell him we've got the shots, we were there, man, we were there. We'll call a press

148

conference, interview the president."

Frank took Charlie by the arm and whispered in his ear, "Take it easy, Charlie. We don't know what's going to happen next."

"Exactly," said Charlie, "That's what's great. This is for real. This isn't yesterday's newspaper. It's so tomorrow, man. This is now and it's big, big, big."

Frank wanted to hear what Pemulwuy, Hanuman, the Dolphin and Not-Sheba would accuse this Mr Butcher (which Mr Butcher?) of. *What will they say? Though I suppose I can guess because they've been telling me all along.* But Mr Butcher-the-teacher turned to Frank and said, "When this gets back to your mother, boy, you'll be in trouble. You can say goodbye to the City High School now."

"Your tomato is very red, sir," said Frank.

"What are you talking about, boy?"

"Your chin, sir."

"Get out and send the next boy in."

"Yes, sir," said Frank and walked out.

He walked down the corridor into the front hall and out to the car park. The coach was waiting and a few of the other kids from his class were already there.

"Mrs Morrell and Mr Butcher aren't back yet," said Rasheda.

"Yeah, I know," said Frank.

"How did you get on with your worksheet?"

"Oh no," said Frank, "My worksheet. I left it –" He was confused for a moment and then dashed off the coach, back to the front hall, along the corridor and into the room with the picture of Miss Charlotte and Master William. Mr Butcher, *yes it is the teacher*, was standing there. He had the worksheet in his hand.

"That's my worksheet," said Frank, "I left it there."

"I know you left it there," said Mr Butcher. "What I also know is that it's not been filled in, has it Frank? You haven't learnt a single thing today, have you?"

"Haven't I, sir?"

"Don't be cheeky, boy," said Mr Butcher, "and make your way to the coach. You've disappointed me."

Frank turned to go but then remembered to

glance over his shoulder at the painting. *Has she gone?* He couldn't see her. He wanted to say good-bye. He wanted to see her again. He wanted to see her quite a lot.

"Carry on," said Mr Butcher, pushing Frank on down the corridor towards the front hall. *When I get back to school,* Frank thought, *I'll try and find out more about her ... the internet ... I could do that at least*

... then I could come back and tell her ... yes ... that's it. He stood outside Chiltern House and looked back at it. *Mind you, she never helped me with my work-sheet ...*

About the Author

Michael Rosen is a household name as a result of his popular radio programmes, in addition to being a highly successful poet for both adults and children.

In this book Michael combines his comic talents with his passion for history. Although Michael is more famous for his picture books, his forays into the junior market are always both funny and original.

Michael Rosen lives in Hackney with his family. He has received both the Smarties Prize and the Eleanor Farjeon Award for Services to Children's Books. Michael is also a very popular performer and lecturer, entertaining huge audiences to universal acclaim.

OTHER BOOKS BY BARN OWL YOU MIGHT ENJOY

You're Thinking About Doughnuts

BY MICHAEL ROSEN

£4.99 ISBN 1-903015-030

This is the first book about Frank, the hero of *You're Thinking About Tomatoes*.

In this book Frank has to accompany his mum to the museum where she works as a cleaner. Left all on his own with the exhibits Frank feels very scared. However, when a friendly skeleton comes alive and tells Frank the story of his life, the boy begins to feel better. When all the other objects in the museum follow his example, Frank begins to learn a lot about history and about himself.

A very funny and engaging book.

"Inventive and ingenious" – *The Guardian*

The Boy Who Sprouted Antlers

JOHN YEOMAN

ILLUSTRATED BY QUENTIN BLAKE

£3.99 ISBN 1-903015-19-7

When young Billy Dexter finds that he actually has grown antlers his life changes in some unexpected ways. A charming, humorous story about daring to be different.

A very funny and heart-warming book, with enchanting, witty pictures by the wonderful Quentin Blake.

Vlad The Drac

BY ANN JUNGMAN

£4.99 ISBN 1-903015-22-7

When Judy and Paul get talked into bringing
a tiny vampire from Romania to England,
they have no idea of the trouble they are
storing up. Vlad may be a vegetarian and
harmless but he does like to wander round
the house and can't resist pretending to be a
scary bloodsucker. How long can Paul and
Judy keep him a secret?

"These stories are excellent for young readers."
Nicholas Tucker in *The Rough Guide to
Children's Books*

Vlad The Drac Returns

BY ANN JUNGMAN

£4.99 ISBN 1-903015-34-0

Vlad the Drac, the tiny vegetarian vampire, is back. Now that he is no longer a secret, Vlad wants his photo in the papers every day and to be on TV as much as possible. The vampire's antics to get publicity get him into lots of trouble but when he goes missing everyone is very worried.

"Funny, unpredictable, playful and defiant, Vlad is always an excellent companion," *The Rough Guide to Children's Books.*

Liar, Liar, Pants on Fire!

BY JEREMY STRONG

£4.99 ISBN 1-903015-37-5

Susie Bonner is a town girl right down to
the tips of her toes but Mum has decided to
move to the country and life in a small place is
not to Susie's taste. To keep up her spirits,
BSusie coresponds regularly with her best
friend Marsha with an account of her new life,
but Susie has a vivid imagination and can't
help adding drama to her descriptions.
So when Marsha comes to stay and
sees village life as it really is – well,
things get a bit difficult.

An amusing and perceptive tale from the
master of comedy, Jeremy Strong.

"Guaranteed entertainment!" Lindsay Fraser,
The Glasgow Herald.